LIFE
Accidentally

KATY FATA

Copyright 2020 by Katy Fata

ISBN: 978-1-7772840-0-8 (paperback)
ISBN: 978-1-7772840-1-5 (ebook)

Printed in the United States of America

Cover and interior book design by Asya Blue

For my mom, with lots of love.

Introduction

It was summertime in Montreal, and, at the tender age of sixteen, I was dealing with the usual issues faced by girls my age. I had an aunt living in the United States who visited us on a regular basis. It felt like a hurricane hit the city whenever she came to town. This woman was a natural disaster. And like a natural disaster, she could be both terrifying and eerily beautiful. Those who were smart knew enough to fear her and take cover. But as a young, hormonal, and impressionable teenager, I just didn't stand a chance.

One day my aunt casually mentioned that my mom had a difficult time when she was pregnant with me. She said that my mom was on the pill but somehow got pregnant just the same. The doctors said that I could be born with birth defects because

I had been conceived while my mom was on birth control pills.

I was so hurt and angry. I wasn't wanted. I was a very big mistake. My mom went out of her way to ensure that I wouldn't be born. It was a big deal for a devout Catholic to take the pill when my mom was a young woman, so it just goes to show how much she didn't want me. But for some fucked-up reason, I was conceived just the same.

I eventually got over the anger that I felt toward my mom. Once I put myself in her shoes, I just couldn't be angry anymore. She was a young woman who already had a few kids, with absolutely no help from anyone, not even my dad. Why the hell would she want another kid? She was actually very brave to attempt birth control because, as I mentioned earlier, this was not an easy thing for a devout Catholic woman in those days. Once I understood this, my anger toward her became pity. It's not that she didn't want me; she just couldn't handle having another child. It's more than understandable. It still hurt, though. Right from the get-go, I wasn't wanted or needed in this world. I wasn't necessary. I was born into life accidentally.

If life can be accidental, then maybe love can also accidentally find its way into your life.

1

At least the Doctor Is Hot...

There's a draft in the room. I've been sitting in this chair for what seems like forever, but I can't move too much. Any movement might put me in the trail of that nauseating odor of urine. The patient in the room across from ours is having a bad day and can't seem to make it to the bathroom on time. The staff isn't quick enough to clean up after her. Poor thing. I bet she never imagined that she would be reduced to depending on others to clean up her vomit and soiled clothing. Such is life.

I can't believe I'm here. I feel like I'm in a dream, a very bad dream. My mom has lung cancer. She never smoked a day in her life. She never drank alcohol. She ate well. She went to church regularly, and wouldn't hear of or allow any gossip while in her presence. She raised four children selflessly, and "honored and obeyed" her husband for fifty difficult years of marriage. And *she* gets hit with lung cancer. How can it be? I can't tell you how many times I ask myself this question in a day. She's sleeping now, but she doesn't look like she's resting. She had half of one lung removed. Now you know that's got to hurt. But it could've been much worse. The original diagnosis that she got makes plain old lung cancer look good. Still, I can't shake this lost and out-of-touch feeling that I live with all of the time.

The doctor hasn't been by yet today. I can't wait to see him. My mom is in excruciating pain, lying in a hospital bed, and I'm longing to see her lung specialist. I am awful, I know. But it makes me feel so good to escape my difficult reality right now and imagine being with the good doctor.

He's *so* hot. I am forever grateful to him for operating on my mom. He saved her life. And he's so hot, but I already mentioned that, didn't I? Not sure what I love most about him. I sure do love his lazy, flirtatious smile. I'd love to run my fingers through his short salt-and-pepper hair. Then, of course, there's his piercing stare. You feel like he's looking right through you. It's like he can read what you're thinking, and of course you know what I'm thinking when he's around. I feel like he knows that I get all hot and bothered, and he plays right into it, flashing that sexy, lazy smile of his and looking at me like I'm the only one in the room. When I speak, he really listens to me. At least, that's how he makes me feel. And then there's his voice, OH MY GOD, his voice. I just love to hear him speak. I want to hear him say my name, over and over again.

Speak of the devil. "Hi, Dr. Ferrante," I eagerly blurted out as he entered the tiny room. He just smiled. He briefly looked my way before turning his complete attention toward my mom. He asked her how she was feeling. "*Come sta oggi, Signora Rinaldi?*"

"*Sto bene, grazie*"—"I'm good, thanks," my mom answered in Italian. Oh, did I forget to mention that he speaks Italian beautifully? He's so sexy.

The painkillers were bothering my mom that day. They were making her nauseous. She was also feeling pretty depressed. I guess it's understandable. It's not that easy to accept that you have lung cancer. The surgeon had to remove the upper lobe of her left lung. That was over a week ago now, and she was still in a lot of pain. Dr. Ferrante said to expect a rough recovery, at least for the next four to six weeks. It's not easy, but so much better than what we were originally told. You see, my mom's illness was originally misdiagnosed by another doctor at a different hospital.

About a month and a half ago, my mom went to the emergency room of the closest hospital, the All Saints Hospital in Montreal, as she was experiencing excruciating pain in her chest and neck. Once at the hospital, they determined that she was not having a heart attack, as originally believed by all. Rather, chest x-rays showed that she had a "spot" on her left lung. More tests, mainly a nuclear scan, revealed abnormal cells in her bones. The doctor immediately determined that my mom had lung cancer, and that it had metastasized to her bones. They told us that she had six to twelve months to live and that we needed to look into palliative care. All of this happened within a matter of about four days. To make matters a little more overwhelming, the doctor told us that the hospital was not equipped to provide treatment for cancer, so we needed to find a doctor at another hospital that had the facilities to treat the cancer. And this was where Dr. Ferrante entered my life.

My mom's diagnosis made no sense at all to me. How could such a huge diagnosis be made so quickly?

I almost immediately believed, in my heart, that things would be OK. I felt that it was Divine Intervention that led my mom to the ER on that awful night. Had she not experienced the pain that was believed to be a heart attack, she would not have gone to the hospital, and the tumor that had placed itself in the upper lobe of her left lung would have continued to go undetected until one day, maybe one year from now, my mom would begin to exhibit symptoms of this silent killer. It would have exposed itself only once it would take possession of other parts of her body.

At the risk of sounding like a religious freak, it really was my faith in God that saved me from losing complete touch with reality.

I prayed, day and night, that there must be a mistake. I knew that my mom was sick, and that it was serious. I also hoped for, and asked God for, what I believed should be the "worst case scenario." I felt that my mom probably had lung cancer. But I asked God to make it operable. I prayed that it had not spread to her bones, or anywhere else for that matter. I also asked everyone that I knew to pray. If there's anything that I've learned in life, it's that you should never underestimate the power of prayer.

Dr. Ferrante examined my mother's incision and told her that everything looked good. "Beautiful" was the word that he used. It always killed me the way doctors, or anyone in the medical industry, liked to describe incisions as "beautiful" upon examination. I mean, really?

I always felt so giddy when Dr. Ferrante was around. I felt like a gauche, horny teenager. I admired him so much. I loved the way he was so focused and professional when he would examine my mom. I also loved the way his body seemed to relax and he would flash that lazy smile at me once the exam was over and he finally directed his attention to me. We seemed to understand each other perfectly. He could just look at me, with his deep, piercing dark eyes, and I was his. We were in a busy hospital, in a tiny room with my poor, sick mom lying in bed, but I was only aware of *him* next to me. On that late afternoon, when the good doctor finally came by to make his rounds, he told me how he felt about me, and I nearly died.

After he examined my mom, he turned to me and said, "You know, Briana, your mom is very lucky to have you." As I struggled to keep myself from wrapping my arms around his neck, right there in that tiny hospital room in front of my mom's bed, I just looked at him, unable to voice my confusion over his statement. I was mesmerized by his dark eyes. His deep stare left me feeling like a little lamb staring back at a beautiful, fierce lion. Towering over me, he gently took my hand with his strong one. He continued, "Not everyone is lucky enough to have someone look after them the way that you look after your mom. You really love her, and you're always by her side. That's special. *You are special.*"

It felt so good to hear him speak to me and to hear such positive words about me leave his seductive, full lips. Of course, it would have felt even better if he'd planted those sexy lips on mine.

I wanted to run my fingers through his salt-and-pepper hair. I would've fucked him right there and then! But he then quickly turned away from me and was gone before I could scrape my tongue off the floor.

By that time, visiting hours were over and I needed to get home. The drive home from the hospital is always difficult, and this day was no different. I can't help but feel so empty. I love my kids so much, but there's something inside of me that's missing. I don't feel alive anymore. I really feel like without my mom, I have nobody to love me. It must be all of the years spent with my husband that totally messed me up. I can't believe that I'm still in this situation.

When I arrived at home that night after spending all day at the hospital, Peter was waiting for me at the front door.

"Why are you back so late? Really, Briana, you know I have a hockey game tonight! Now, thanks to you, I have to run every red light just to get there on time. You're such a selfish person."

Over the years I learned that it's just easier not to answer back because it will avoid an ugly argument. And I was just too tired. And I had my kids to think about.

"Where are the kids?"

"They're in bed." Peter quickly gathered his hockey equipment and left within minutes.

He didn't even ask how my mom was doing.

The next day I was back at the hospital, bright and early. I had just missed the doctor, though. Apparently, he came by to see my mom very early. He told her that everything looked good, and that she could leave the hospital the following morning. He didn't come by for the rest of the day. What a letdown. My mom did mention that he asked about me.

She told me that he asked her where the "young lady" was, in Italian. "*La signorina non e arrivata ancora?*" To which my mom answered, "*Ma che signorina? Quella e una donna sposata con due figli piccoli.*" "Young lady? She's a married woman with two young children." He apparently didn't respond to her comment. *Way to go, Mom! Thanks!* Somehow, my mom, God love her, never seemed to have my back.

This morning, the day of my mom's dismissal from the hospital, I got there bright and early, only to find her dressed and ready to go home. My mom's bag, which contained the few toiletries that she brought with her to the hospital, was all packed. Apparently, the nurse had helped her get dressed. I was so happy to see her this way, because it meant that she was starting to feel better. It had been ten days since the cancer had been removed by "Dr. Sexy Pants." We just needed to wait for the doctor to come by, examine her, and sign the release papers.

Well, the doctor finally did make an appearance, by early afternoon. He was kind and polite and very professional with my mom. However, he didn't send any sexy, sensuous smiles my way. Hell, he hardly looked at me! He almost looked a little annoyed by my presence. Was I imagining this as well? I got the feeling that he was a little upset because he learned of my marital status, and may have felt a little misled by me. Could it be? Was I being my usual neurotic self? If the doctor was indeed a little annoyed with me, well, did he have every reason to feel this way? I did flirt with him, true. I'm sure he felt how drawn to him I was. My body language, the way that I smiled shyly at him, the way that I laughed at anything even remotely funny that he would say, well, it all sent the message that I was definitely into him. And, yes, I am married with kids. But how was he to know what kind of marriage I have? He didn't know that I would give anything to be out of the situation that I am in. Well, the good doctor isn't entirely innocent either. He is also married. And unless I am mistaken, he was sending me the same sexual vibes that I've been sending his way. *Unless I am mistaken...*

Dr. Ferrante told my mom that he would see her in a month's time and that she should call his office should the need arise. He then gave me a little nod and was gone. I felt so confused. I think I wanted to cry. But why? Because the doctor didn't pay any attention to me and I felt snubbed? Or maybe it was because I had to face the reality that I had probably just imagined any chemistry between us? Or maybe because I wouldn't see him for a good month's time? I wanted to cry, but I just couldn't. I mean, *really*? I had cried so many tears over my mom's illness in the past month. How silly to shed tears because the man that I had the hots for didn't feel the same way about me. It's just that I felt so sexy around Dr. Ferrante. He awakened feelings in me that had been dormant for years. *He doesn't want me.* I am so used to not getting any affection, so why expect some now? It still hurt, though.

2

Sweet 16

I met my husband when I was just sixteen years old. I was too young, very sweet and naïve. How stupid that girl seems to me now. I loved Peter, as much as a sixteen-year-old is able to truly love. Peter came from a very dysfunctional family. Hey, I'm not saying that my family was perfect, but Peter's family was exceptionally dysfunctional. His father was an abusive alcoholic who constantly fought with his mom, verbally and physically. He has three siblings, two of whom are probably the nastiest people that I've ever met in my life. He also seemed to surround himself with a group of "friends" that had the same background as himself, with the same set of family problems, and with the same mean genes as his awful siblings. But back then, Peter wasn't as mean and messed up as the rest of them. He would tell me all the time that he had such a difficult childhood, and that he did not want to be the kind of man that his dad was. I felt sorry for him, and I wanted to take his pain away. I believed that he was a good person and that he wanted a better life for himself. We dated throughout high school, and then college and university. He was my first and only boyfriend. I was committed to our relationship, and loyal to him to the end.

I was very sweet in those days. *I was a good girl, I was.* I studied most of the time, and I was in business school. I also worked part-time to pay for my tuition and books. I saw Peter whenever I could, which was on most weekends. Right from the beginning, he did things that bothered me, but I was so tolerant of all of his faults. Heaven knows, I had so many faults of my own, so how could I hold his against him? Well, how stupid of me and how naïve. I didn't know that you should carefully examine your boyfriend's faults in order to determine if you think that you can live with them forever.

"Why don't you love me?" I stood in front of the mirror and half expected it to tell me what I was doing wrong.

My sixteen-year-old self didn't like looking in that harsh, unforgiving mirror that stood between the two single beds in the room that I shared with my sister.

The shame and guilt so deeply embedded in my soul forced me to stare and take the brutal daily inventory of what I believed was my cross to bear. The girl in the mirror was always so critical and quick to let me know what until now only Peter had been honest enough to tell me.

"At least my hair is long, and that's OK. Everyone has long hair nowadays. Mommy always says that I get my strawberry-blonde hair from her side of the family." The girl who looked back at me shrugged her shoulders and then looked away.

My mom always seemed to be proud of the fact that I had inherited some traits from her side of the family. I guess it just made me happy to please my mom in any way. And that's not all that I inherited from mom's genes. To my horror, I also got the ample bosom that seemed to be bestowed upon all the women in my mom's family. I was always so shy, and at sixteen years old I didn't welcome all the disgusting smirks from depraved teens who always had "boobies" on their mind.

Peter seemed to have a preference for brunettes. He would always go on about how sexy brunettes are. He told me that his old girlfriend Selena had beautiful long, dark hair. Apparently, she was an exotic beauty. He even called her "Barbie."

I remember feeling so put out by that.

Once, I cheekily turned to Peter and said, "Well now, Peter, I think that I'm the one who looks a little like all the Barbie dolls that I still have packed in boxes in my basement. At least I have the right color of hair!"

It was so silly of me, I know, but I couldn't help what I was feeling. *If anyone is going to be compared to Barbie, then damn it, it should be me and not Selena!*

That asshole casually said, "No, Briana. You're cute, but you could never be beautiful. It's just not you."

3

A Sopressata and a Capocollo in Exchange for Lung Surgery

My mom's appointment with Dr. Ferrante was quickly approaching. I was dying to see him. I knew what I wanted to wear. I had picked out a new wraparound jean dress. It looked professional, yet feminine. It showed off my curves without making it seem too obvious. I paired it with open-toe, sling-back, brown-leather high-heeled sandals. I wore my hair loose, straightened, of course, and a pinkish lip gloss to help accentuate my lips. I wanted my lips to look "kissable."

The dress was one of the first things I had bought for myself in ages. After I had my kids, I felt so self-conscious about my body that I didn't feel "worthy" of having nice things. So I never really shopped for myself. I really let myself go. It didn't help that I was only working part-time. I really could no longer afford the things that I liked.

My attraction for Dr. Ferrante awoke feelings in me that had died a long time ago. I felt sexual again and wanted to look good. So, I finally took some time and went shopping for myself.

I lost about ten pounds when my mom got sick. I definitely looked leaner, but I still felt so "loose." I really needed to exercise and firm up a little. At least my breasts were still nice. Gravity hadn't gotten the better of them, *yet*.

We had been waiting about two hours before we actually got to see Dr. Ferrante on the morning of my mom's appointment. My sister and one of my brothers also came to the appointment. The doctor was always very busy, and a long wait before actually seeing him was to be expected. I couldn't believe that my brother brought the doctor a *capocollo* and *a sopressata*. My family is originally from Southern Italy, and *capocollo* and *sopressata* are two traditional dry-cured cold cuts from the Calabria region. By the way, Dr. Ferrante's family is originally from the same region of Italy as my family. According to my brother, he heard from a good "source" that the doctor really liked Italian salami. So, when my dad learned this, well, he just had to send him some that he'd personally made at home. I know that the gesture was nice, but come on, *salami*? I felt so embarrassed. I felt like we were in a Sofia Loren movie from the sixties, and we were using the barter system to exchange goods and services.

I spotted the doctor right away. I could have spotted him a mile away, even in a dark, crowded room. It was a little shocking for me to realize just how much his striking good looks could literally take my breath away.

We locked eyes for a moment. He smiled at me with that way of his, and then he said hello to the rest of my family. *Of course, this appointment was all about me, right?* In light conversation before the exam, the doctor mentioned that he had had a very bad week. He had apparently lost a couple of patients that had undergone lung transplants. He looked so broken up about it. *And still, he has the courage to keep on trying to help the many desperate and broken-hearted patients that turn to him in hopes of a miracle.*

Dr. Ferrante then reviewed my mom's latest x-rays and advised her that the pathology report indicated that chemotherapy was not required. The cancer was removed, along with the tumor that had decided to take over the upper lobe of her left lung. "Dr. Sexy Pants" ripped the vile bastard from my mom's chest and destroyed it.

The size of the tumor was about two centimeters. It wasn't a very big tumor, and from what I read from the internet, larger tumors tend to be more dangerous in general. This certainly answers the age-old question. *Oh, come on.* We all know that size matters. And sometimes less is not more. It's just less.

I asked the doctor about the possibility and necessity of screening for lung cancer. My mom had lung cancer, and she never smoked a day in her life. So is it genetic? The doctor said that a recent report in the *New England Journal of Medicine* indicated that studies are now showing that there are benefits to screening for lung cancer through the use of CT.

I realized that the topic of discussion was indeed a very serious one, but all I could focus on was how sexy his lips were.

I wanted so badly to speak to the doctor in private. I wanted it to be just the two of us. With everyone around, well, I couldn't freely flirt with him.

"Doctor, the other day I read an interesting article in the *New England Journal of Medicine* on the great health benefits of using marijuana."

He looked a little stunned. "Wow, you read the *New England Journal of Medicine?*"

"Sure I do." I tried to keep a straight face. I guess his reaction should've insulted me. But who was I kidding? "Actually, I may have read it in *Cosmo.*"

Dr. Ferrante's eyes widened in shock, and then he burst out laughing.

After we left, I just couldn't stop thinking about Dr. Ferrante. He was so broken up over losing a couple of his patients. I had such a need to comfort him, and this feeling stayed with me throughout the whole day. Later that evening, I decided that I would text him. He did, after all, give out his mobile phone number. If he didn't want anyone to contact him via his cell phone, then he wouldn't have given out his number in the first place, right?

So I finally wrote:

Dr. Ferrante, you are so gifted and courageous. You continue to help so many people that need you, even though you sometimes have bad days that would prevent the average person from moving forward. Pretty special indeed! Can't thank you enough for everything. You are firmly placed in my heart forever. Thank you.

I felt like a schoolgirl.

A couple of hours later I heard my phone alert me to an incoming text, and I just knew that it was from HIM. He wrote:

Hi, Briana, thank you for the kind words. You are also a special person and your mother is quite fortunate to have you. Remember to check the article that I told you about regarding the benefits of screening for lung cancer...speak to you soon. Alex

I spent the next few days planning for an upcoming business trip to Chicago. But all I could think about was Dr. Ferrante. I thought about him continuously. I wanted so badly to hear his voice.

After my son turned a year old, I really needed to get a job because I was running out of money. I took a part-time marketing job for a high-end chocolate company. The job was flexible, and I basically worked out of my home office. I didn't make much money, but the job allowed me to really be around my kids a lot. It also required me to occasionally travel for business.

Needless to say, my trip wasn't exactly productive. I found myself thinking about Dr. Ferrante constantly. He was always on my mind. On the plane ride to Chicago, I read the article that he had referred to on the benefits of screening for lung cancer. I guess thinking about him so much gave me an idea.

About a day after arriving home, in the late afternoon, I texted the good doctor once again. I wrote:

> It is encouraging that studies are now showing that there is a benefit to screening for lung cancer. I'm a female who has never smoked and I don't want to be part of the increasing percentage of non-smoking females who gets lung cancer. However, should the need arise, you need to promise me that you'll do me...my lungs of course. It would be thrilling to leave my "chest" in the hands of the Wayne Gretzky of pulmonary medicine.

I had read a magazine article on Dr. Ferrante when I sat in his waiting room. The article referred to him as the "Wayne Gretzky" of his field. *Oh, there is no doubt that he is the great one!*

Almost immediately after sending my text, I felt an uneasy feeling come over me. How could I send such a message, filled with such sexual innuendo? What would he think of me? I basically sent my mom's doctor a text telling him to call me should he feel like having sex with me! It was so funny to me before I sent it. But once I actually sent it, well, it still was a little funny, but a little scary as well depending on how Dr. Ferrante would take it.

I didn't receive a response and had a sleepless night. As much as I wanted the doctor so badly, I felt embarrassed over my behavior. So I decided to send Dr. Ferrante another text.

I wrote:

> *Please forgive my last text to you. I blame exhaustion, as it prevented me from keeping my dreams from slipping into my reality. I am just way too inappropriately familiar with you, probably because you have pretty much taken over my dreams in the last couple of months. I am so sorry, and I am mortified.*

It didn't take the doctor too long to respond to this text. He wrote:

> *Not to worry, Briana. As I have already said you are a special person with a charming personality!! I'm not in the least offended. Hope your mom is well. AF.*

He signed off with his initials, AF, Alex Ferrante. At least he didn't sign off using his "Dr." title. And being the moron that I am, well I just couldn't resist sending a response to his last text.

I wrote:

OK now, I won't be held responsible for what comes out of my mouth when you go on like that! My mom is well, thanks. She misses you though...it must be that smile of yours, or maybe it's your voice...Nope, not responsible.

4

Happy Is the Bride the Sun Shines on

About one week before my wedding day, my husband dropped a pretty big bomb on me. He told me that he had a gambling problem, and that he owed some loan sharks over $20,000. He was asking me to pay for his debt. I was shocked, disappointed, and disgusted. He knew how much I disliked gambling. My brother had a gambling problem that destroyed his marriage and hurt my family like you have no idea. So to find out that my future husband had the same problem, well, it really hurt me. What hurt even more was that I was totally clueless. The man that was supposed to be my best friend had hid so much from me. Our relationship was a complete lie.

I went through with the wedding. I couldn't even look at him because I just saw a liar. My mom advised me to forgive him, as did my sister and some friends of mine. Peter told me that he was done with gambling, and that he would make it up to me. So I decided to go through with it, although I knew in my heart that I was doing the wrong thing. I stood in front of God, with a very heavy heart, and married the man that I knew I should not marry. I still remember how difficult it was for me to say my vows. I felt pain with every word that came out of my mouth, and it took all that I had to keep my quiet tears from turning into violent sobs. I understood only too well that I had just embarked on a very difficult and painful voyage.

To say that our relationship has been rocky is an understatement. Peter did absolutely nothing to make it up to me. He continued to live his life as he had prior to getting married. The only difference was that once I actually lived with him, I saw things about his behavior that he had always kept hidden from me. He would go out a lot and get back home in the wee hours of the morning. He would always be very vague about his whereabouts. We argued continuously. He even told me that he did not "answer to me." Silly me, I thought that married couples did answer to each other. I was so unhappy and I felt so trapped. I felt like I had nobody to turn to for support.

I also had Peter's family to contend with. Peter's brother is such a loser. He's just a mean person. He's bitter and jealous and wants everyone around him to be as miserable as he is. He hated me from the very beginning. I think it was because he wanted what I had. He envied my safe, happy childhood in a good, stable home with parents and siblings that loved me. Peter's loser brother always "whispered" insulting things about me when I was around. He would speak low enough that he wasn't actually speaking right to me, but loud enough that I could hear what he was saying. He was such a coward.

I put an end to the creep's abusive behavior toward me on the first Christmas day after my wedding. Peter and I went to his parents' for Christmas lunch. I heard the asshole's cowardly voice right on cue, as soon as I walked in the door.

"That bitch finally decided to make an entrance. It took her long enough to get here."

It really wasn't anything that I hadn't already heard coming out of his vile mouth on many occasions. But somehow, on that day, well, I just couldn't leave it be.

I casually walked into the kitchen, looked that piece of shit right in the face, and said, "You know, if you have anything to say about me, then go right ahead and say it to me. Don't be such a coward and whisper it behind my back."

Well, the low-life went crazy and basically

threw any insult that he could think of at me. I remember feeling struck by the fact that nobody there, not his parents and not his other siblings, stepped in and told him to stop it. They all felt that this behavior was OK. That's how dysfunctional they are.

Peter's brother looked at me with sheer hatred in his eyes. His words were dripping with venom. "I dream of the day when I will see you all bloody, lying dead somewhere on a dark street."

I remember feeling like I had been punched in the stomach. He went on to say that if he won the lottery, he would pay Peter to leave me. That was when Peter burst out laughing. And that's when I left that disgusting home. I couldn't believe that Peter laughed at such hateful words that were directed at me. He didn't defend me, nor did he tell his loser brother to fuck off. He laughed. And I just wanted to die. I was so hurt. I hated them all.

After that, I hardly ever went by my in-laws and I rarely attended any of their family gatherings. I told Peter that I did not marry him to endure his family's abuse. I'd already had enough abuse from Peter alone to last me a lifetime. Of course his family told people that I was just awful because I hardly went by and I wasn't a good daughter-in-law. They never did mention to anyone, though, why I didn't go by much.

Needless to say, this didn't help my marriage. I buried myself in my work. I wanted to leave Peter, but I didn't have the courage to do it. I don't know why. Maybe it was because I felt like getting divorced meant that I was a failure at something. I should've understood that getting divorced was the first step toward getting my life back. I also still felt a sense of loyalty toward Peter. After all of the lies and the abuse, I still loved him. I still believed that Peter could be that good person that I believed him to be for so many years when we were dating. But it was like fighting a losing battle with Peter. Work kept me away a lot of the time, and it suited me just fine. It's what kept me sane.

After about four years of living this way, my biological clock started ticking. I really wanted kids. I gave up my "real" job when I was trying to get pregnant. I worked in marketing for a telecommunications company. My job required long hours and monthly business travel. It suited me just fine when I was married with no kids. But I knew that I could not be the kind of mom that I wanted to be and the kind of employee that this position needed me to be at the same time. So after trying to conceive unsuccessfully for two years, I left my job. I finally got pregnant with my son, Marco, one month later.

I had received a blessing and I couldn't have been happier. But, naturally, Peter's stench surrounded me. Once again, I could feel his darkness shade the sunshine that had come into my life.

After the birth of my beautiful boy, I learned that Peter owed a loan shark about $50,000. I'd felt that something was up for a while, but every time I confronted Peter, he denied that anything was wrong. He accused me of nagging him and stressing him out. I was so disgusted with him, and it made me sick to be around him. But I also desperately wanted to give Marco a sibling. My biological clock was ticking loud and clear, so I forgave him once again and made procreation my mission. Miraculously, less than two years later, I was once again blessed with a child, this time a beautiful baby girl. Her name is Elisa.

I wasn't in love with Peter, and I hadn't been in years. I still felt love for him, though. I guess I can best explain it by describing it as the kind of love that a mother feels for a child of hers that has done something really bad, like committed a crime. You don't stop caring about a person even if that person has done something wrong. However, I also felt hate for him. The hate was inevitable after the many years of lies, betrayals, disappointments, and regrets. I should've left Peter before the hate.

The last time that I had sex with Peter was when Elisa was only six months old. One night Peter stumbled into our room in the wee hours, reeking of alcohol. I told him that if he wanted to continue to share my bed, he had to stop going out wherever it was that he went and getting home late, drunk. Needless to say, that's when we stopped sharing the same bed.

Over the years, I wondered how a man could go on for so long without sex. All you ever hear about on television or in magazines is how men are just so sex starved. *Silly, naïve little me.* I finally realized that just because he wasn't having sex with me, well it didn't mean that he wasn't having sex with someone else. I asked him on several occasions if he was sleeping around. He always denied it, of course. I didn't believe him, but I didn't do anything about it either.

I like to think that my kids are the reason why I was brought together with Peter. You could not find a worse match than Peter and me if you tried, but together we made the most awesome, intelligent, beautiful kids. I guess I can say that they made all the abuse worth it in the end. Still, I could've lived my whole life without experiencing any of the ugliness that was brought into my life because of Peter. I have so many regrets, and there's so much pain in my heart. Living this way for so long is exhausting. It will kill a person's spirit.

5

Quit While You're Ahead

My favorite uncle was diagnosed with liver cancer, and he went to see Dr. Ferrante for a second opinion.

Unfortunately, the doctor could not provide him with any positive new information. My uncle is living with cancer, and God willing he will be able to live without pain for as long as possible.

My cousin went to the appointment with her dad, and she called me up on the phone afterwards. She let me know how it all went, and she told me how disappointed she was that nothing could really be done to help her dad. In an instant, our life as we know it can become a nightmare. We truly need to be grateful for and cherish every good moment in life. It is a shame that we often only realize how good things are and how good we have it when we risk losing a loved one.

And on a more shallow note, my cousin told me that the doctor mentioned me during the visit. He apparently said that I easily freak out, and that I overreact and that I worry too much. *Me*, overreact? Why, that's just absurd.

I, of course, spent countless hours obsessing over the doctor's comment. It just felt so good that he actually referred to me. It meant that I was on his mind. It was obvious that *I* wanted to play "doctor" with an actual doctor. But what was *he* doing?

I am not sure what it was that made me make my next move, but I really wish I had not done what I did.

Stupid, stupid me. I wanted to take advantage of this opening to have more contact with Dr. Ferrante. I figured that the best way was to text him again.

I wrote:

So, I easily freak out eh? OK Wayne....I mean Dr. Ferrante. Actually, the only thing that freaks me out these days is a really good-looking, suave, charming and a little sarcastic lung doctor that I met during my mom's recent hospitalization. I think he must really be a witch doctor who specializes in love potions!!!

He almost immediately responded with a text

of his own. He wrote:

> *Hey Briana-witty as ever I see!! Nice seeing you the other day. Should come by more often... you add zest to my day with your references from the New England Journal of Medicine!! :)*

I thought I was going to have a heart attack. I should've left well enough alone, but I always have to take it one step further and ruin everything. This time, I wrote:

> *Ooohhh...you think I'm zesty. Interesting how your mind took you to thinking of "flavor, tasty, spicy" when you thought of me. So you like my references? As brilliant as you are, I'm pretty sure that I could teach you a few things. A cold shower sounds real good right about now. How will I go about my day now? At least I don't need to rip out any vital organs. Vital Organs...ooohhh...now you probably need a cold shower!*

Another immediate response:

> *If this keeps up, we're both in trouble...I'm off to surgery-hope I can concentrate...!!! Speak to you soon and let me know if you need something. Alex :)*

So this is really where I should've just quit while I was ahead:

> *OK, I'll let you know if I need something, Alex. Alex...AAlex...AAAlex...AAAAlex...AAAAAlex... AAH...AAH...AAH...ALEX!*#*&@ I need a cigarette...*

No response. How mortifying. I went too far. I don't understand it. It sounded so funny when I thought to write it, but it immediately stopped being funny as soon as I sent it.

Much later that evening I did finally get a response from him. He wrote:

You need more than a cigarette.

No sign off. His response was very dry, and I could feel how turned off he was.

I was so embarrassed and hurt. I also felt a little angry. I was confused. My last text was indeed in poor taste, but I was kidding. I felt that he had given me as much as I gave to him. So why the sudden change of tone? His response cut like a knife. I was suddenly the foolish little girl who crossed the line with the great doctor.

I didn't sleep at all that night. A mix between embarrassment and a little bit of anger set my cheeks on fire. *How did I get myself into this mess?* I wondered. I'd disgraced myself and my family. *What must he think of me?* Well, obviously not very much.

Very early the next morning I decided that apologizing was the right thing to do. I wrote:

Sorry, keep forgetting who you are. You seem to bring out a warped sense of humor in me. Don't understand it, but it won't happen again.

No sign off from me either.
He simply responded with:

Don't worry about it.

Again, no sign off.

I need to at all costs stay away from this man. He is like a drug for me. No, he's more like the really delicious chocolate that I can't resist when I'm premenstrual! *He's irresistible, and I can't keep it all together around him.*

Making a fool out of myself is one thing, but how could I do this to my mom? I don't want my behavior to reflect poorly on her. She still needs him to be her doctor, and he is the best in his field.

I really needed to get a grip on reality and take charge of my life again. I couldn't allow myself to be taken over by grief anymore and use it as an excuse to act like a foolish schoolgirl. I think the doctor's cool, disdainful response was just the wake-up call that I needed. But in the moment, it just hurt so much.

So, after another sleepless night, I decided that I needed to make big changes in my life: embrace the positives in my life and work on the negatives. I am a good mom, at least I used to be, and I will be once again. I am a strong woman, somewhere deep inside of me. I am smart, even if my brain could use a battery change. I am good-looking, behind my haggard appearance. I have not lived my life to the fullest. I have not used all the positive gifts that God gave me to allow me to make the very most out of my life. I am not the very best that I can be. This needs to change.

Whenever I have felt like my life is just too difficult to handle, God has been there for me. God has been my parent, my friend, my therapist, and my teacher. God has listened without judgment. Through God, I gained the strength to overcome difficult times, and I am so grateful for my faith as it has seen me through sometimes impossible circumstances.

Am I a religious freak? I don't think so. I don't even take part in any of the customs of my religion. I do, however, deeply love God. I cling to my faith and trust that it will get me through difficult times, especially when there's nobody or no place to really turn to. Isn't that ultimately what religion and our faith are there for?

6

Seek and You Shall Find

I sn't it funny and sometimes a little scary the way things work out in life? There really is more to it than just what's around us that we can see in this life. There has to be, because I really don't know how else to explain it. There is a higher power. I also feel that there are people that we love that have passed on to the next chapter of existence and are still out there, looking out for us. For me, I feel that my paternal grandmother is looking out for me. I loved her so much and I just know that when I speak to her in my mind, she can actually hear me. It doesn't really matter if this is true or not, because what matters is how I feel and what I believe to be true.

When my mom got sick, I felt like it was just surreal. I knew from the very beginning that my mom was very sick, but I also believed in my heart that she would get over it. When Dr. Ferrante contacted me to advise that the cancer had not spread to her bones, as previously diagnosed, I felt like I was having a dream. I had dreamt of being told that my mom's condition was misdiagnosed so often that I couldn't determine if I was still dreaming when I was speaking with the doctor on the phone. It didn't help that the doctor's voice was so familiar to me and I didn't know why. At the time of that call, I had only spoken to the doctor twice before, but when I spoke to him on the phone, it felt like the voice at the other end of the receiver was coming from an old friend or someone I knew very intimately. So this really contributed to the "dream-like" state that I had fallen into.

From the very beginning, I felt an extremely close connection to Dr. Ferrante. I felt like I knew him well, like we were close. I was definitely drawn to him. I began to feel like maybe we knew each other in a previous life.

Do we feel the connection if we come across a person that we were once intimately close to in a previous life? Maybe we do, if the relationship that we had with that person was so close or deep. Maybe I did intimately know Dr. Ferrante in a previous life, because I sure feel like there is a deep connection with him. But maybe that's just my "lust" talking!

The whole texting fiasco with Dr. Ferrante was over one year ago. So much has happened to me since then, and my life has changed drastically.

First of all, my husband left me. Can you believe it? He just didn't come home one day. I found a letter from Peter on the dresser explaining why he had to leave. He apparently had gotten into trouble again with a loan shark. He had accumulated a huge amount of debt and could no longer make the mortgage payments or pay any of the bills. He wrote that we were all better off without him and that we needed to get a divorce.

Well, there was no doubt that we were all better off without him. However, what about my children? They are unaware of how troubled their dad is, and they really love him. Having to explain to Marco and Elisa that their dad had left us was by far the hardest thing that I have ever done.

I finally explained to them that their dad wasn't well and he needed to leave to get better. He needed to go away so that he could fix whatever was wrong with him.

My kids asked me every day if their dad was coming home. And I would always respond by telling them that Peter loved them dearly and he would come back when he was well again. They finally stopped asking after a few months, but they still talk about him on occasion.

When Marco has difficulty with something, like with one of his toys or with an electronic game, he still says things like, "Maybe Daddy will be able to fix it when he gets back." And Elisa will say things like, "Do you remember when Daddy used to make cupcakes with us?" I can't tell you how much it breaks my heart. I would do anything to take away any pain that my kids feel. I thought that every parent felt this way about their kids. Maybe Peter doesn't feel this way. Maybe he does, but he just doesn't know how to be a better dad. After all, he had such a rough childhood and he never really saw what a good dad is all about. I don't want to feel sorry for him, but I can't hate him entirely either. I just can't do that to my kids.

Why do we stay in situations that are wrong for us, even toxic? I was unhappily married to my husband for years, and I dated him unhappily for years before that. When I was younger I just didn't know any better. I didn't quite get it that I should be treated better. When I first got married, it was really rough. Even though I understood that it wasn't a good union, I was afraid of leaving the marriage for fear that I wouldn't find someone else to love and marry before it would be too late to have kids. And then once I had the kids, well, I just couldn't do it to them. I wanted my kids to grow up with two parents that lived together. Truthfully, I am and always have been a coward, and I'm afraid of being alone. I would rather be miserable with someone than be alone.

I really needed to leave Peter a long time ago. We were so awful together and truly brought out the worst in each other. We have mostly been so unhappy together. I just didn't know how to do it without hurting my children.

In my heart, I wanted so desperately to be free of him. That's why I say that things have a way of somehow working out. I didn't have the courage to leave him, so he finally left me. I guess I need to be grateful to him for this at least. But I won't go so far as sending him any thank you cards. It's been rough and emotional, but liberating.

My kids coped fairly well considering that a divorce is really traumatizing for anyone, especially young children. I guess it helped that so many of their school friends are in similar situations. That made things seem a little more normal for them. Isn't it so sad to be grateful that there are so many divorced parents? Yes, it's real sad, but it's true.

Apart from feeling guilty for not being able to give my kids the kind of family life that I had always dreamed about, I was struggling to pay the many debts and bills that I had been left with. I couldn't do it. I didn't make enough money to pay for the mortgage, property taxes, utilities, groceries, activities for the kids, and so forth. I had quickly gone through any savings that I still had. I didn't want to lose the house. After losing so much, I really didn't want my children to lose the only home that they had ever lived in. Just when I thought that I had no choice but to give up, my prayers were answered.

Actually, I have to say that I don't like to bother God with problems that don't have to do with health, so I never actually asked God to fix my financial situation. However, God must've just known, and he came through for me yet again.

I ran into my old English professor from high school one day at the supermarket. I always loved Mrs. Delia because she was so interesting and full of life. I have such fond memories of studying in her classes. I loved reading anything and everything that came my way. Not only did we discuss classics by Shakespeare in her class, but I fondly remember reading great books like *The Catcher in the Rye*, *The Outsiders*, *The Apprenticeship of Duddy Kravitz*, and my all-time favorite, *Jane Eyre*.

Mrs. Delia asked me to join her for a coffee in the coffee shop next door to the supermarket. We sat and chatted for such a long time, catching up on what life had sent our way since I took her class over twenty years earlier. I guess I was feeling nostalgic and a little emotional, because I just broke down in tears and purged what I had been keeping inside of me for so long. I didn't have anyone to really confide in. I couldn't burden my mom with the details of my life, because she had to concentrate on taking care of her health. The few friends that I had left had too much drama of their own to provide me with any real support. I was on my own, and it was so hard. So seeing dear Mrs. Delia was really a godsend.

It turns out that Mrs. Delia works for an online specialty magazine as a writer and editor. She told me that she had been looking for someone to write a weekly column on sexual fantasies. It didn't pay much, but it would sure help me pay some bills. I have to admit that I was a little surprised, but I was also excited and grateful to Mrs. Delia for offering me the job.

So that's how I began to write about sexual fantasies in a weekly column, and that's also the way that I got to keep my home.

I don't really make too much money. I could leave my present job and go back to a professional, higher-paying corporate job, but that would also mean going back to a life where my job has to be my top priority. Marco and Elisa need me now, so most of my time has to be with them. To be with them, I sacrifice the latest fashions and expensive vacations. Those things are nice to have, not must-haves.

I kept my word and stayed away from Dr.

Ferrante. I didn't accompany my mother to her follow-up visits with the doctor, and that was actually the hardest part. I wanted to be with my mom, but I couldn't show up with her at her visits. I couldn't face Dr. Ferrante after my last embarrassing text to him. I didn't know how he'd react if he saw me again. What if he thought of me as a stalker? Cowardly as ever!

7

One Door Closes, Kick Another One Open

I was in the parking lot of the local Costco loading my car full of bulk item "household essentials" when I met one of the strangest people to ever come into my life.

My head was deep into the trunk of the car as I tried to squeeze in all of the packages that I had just bought, when a deep, rough male voice called my name. "Hello, Briana." His voice was so deep, and he said my name so low, so slow, that I felt a shiver run through my body. I had leaned so deep into the trunk that I practically had to pull my body out. "Hello" was my simple response. I didn't know this man, but I instantly felt like he was trouble. He was tall, with dark wavy hair and light-gray eyes. He was very broad-shouldered and very fit. His nose was a little crooked, and he had a couple of deep scars on the left side of his forehead just above his eye.

"I'm sorry, but do I know you?"

"No, but you will because you see, Briana, we are going to become very good friends."

OK, he scared the hell out of me, and my mind filled with the many emails that I had received over the years warning women of the sick sexual predators lurking in parking lots waiting for the right moment to attack their unsuspecting prey.

He must've understood that I was about to make a run for it, because he then said in that deep, scary voice of his, "You don't have to be afraid of me, because I don't want to hurt you. But we do need to talk, so stop looking around as if you're going to run away and don't scream like a silly little girl."

Just who the fuck was this guy, anyways?! "What do you want from me, and how do you know my name? And who the hell are you?"

"Well now, you have a little character, don't you? I like that in a girl. OK, honey, my name is Rocco. Your husband owes me quite a bit of money, you know. I was kind enough to lend him some money a while ago, but he isn't as nice as I am. He just took off without paying me back for the loan.

Now, don't you think that it was pretty low of him to just take off like that?"

"Look, he ran off on me as well. I don't know what you're hoping to get from me, but even if I had the money, I sure don't feel like I should pay for Peter's problems. He's not my problem anymore."

"Well, I sure don't appreciate him being my problem either. Look, honey, I get that he's a deadbeat, but you're just gonna have to make good on this. Like it or not, you married the guy, so it's now up to you to pay for it. I'm not going away from your life until you do."

"This is crazy. I don't have any money to give you. "

"Honey, I understand. You need to appreciate that I normally handle these situations differently, but when I learned about you, I just couldn't pass up this opportunity to use your many talents.

Oh my God, was this guy for real? "Look, Rocco, I've got ice cream in my car and it's melting, so I really need to go now."

"Give me the ice cream."

"Why do you want my ice cream?"

He looked a little annoyed and said, "I have a cooler in the trunk of my car. I'll put the ice cream in there while we talk."

Apart from someone taking a road trip, just who the hell keeps a cooler in his car? I'll tell you who, only someone that is up to no good, that's who! Maybe someone who needs to keep body parts on ice, that's who!

"I told you that I need to go now. It's been real…"

He interrupted me and said, "Sweetheart, you need to be smart now, so just listen to what I have to say.

"Are you threatening me?"

"Don't be silly. I don't threaten little girls. I do, however, feel like I have the right to do whatever it takes to Peter, or his face, or his legs, or any other part of his sorry body as payment for the money that he owes me."

"So what you're telling me, Rocco, is that you will hurt Peter if I don't get you the money that he owes you?"

He smirked a little and said, "Not quite, but pretty close."

"What do you mean? Just tell me what you're saying, already! And what makes you think that I give a damn about what you do to Peter? You have no idea what he put me through. He just took money from you. He took much more from me."

"I know enough about you to understand that you love your kids. So you don't want anything bad to happen to the father of your kids, for their sake. You see, Briana, I know that you were a good wife to that guy, and you're a good mother. You will do the right thing."

"But I don't have any money for you." I wanted to cry, but of course I would never cry in front of this character. He was right. I couldn't let Rocco "do whatever he does" to Peter. Oh, I'm not saying that Peter didn't deserve a good beating. But I couldn't allow the father of my children to get hurt by this thug. I love my kids too much to allow them to be hurt like that. Not to mention that it was just wrong."

"OK, tell me how much he owes you, and I'll have to pay you a little bit at a time, because I just don't have anything to give you right now."

"Briana, honey, I told you that I understand your situation. I know that you don't have the money for me. But I was thinking that you could pay off the debt in another way. "

What the fuck! "Oh no, I'm sorry but you're gonna have to do whatever you feel is necessary to Peter and to me, because I just don't roll that way, and—"

He raised his hand to cut me off, then rolled his eyes and said, "Easy, little tiger. Get your mind out of the gutter. I was thinking that you could help me with a little project that I've undertaken."

I couldn't help but think that he used an interesting choice of words. He could actually pass for an undertaker. But I digress.

"Briana, I know that you write for a weekly column. You're really good."

OK... "Thank you. But what does my column have to do with it?"

"I've always wanted to write a book. I just need a little help doing it. I need help putting my thoughts into words. I need help putting my stories together. Help me write my book, and I will consider the debt paid in full."

"But why me? I don't have any training as a writer, and I don't know how to write a book. You can get help from someone who is actually qualified."

"I think that you're qualified because I like your style. You'll do just fine for me, and I don't need or trust anyone else with this. I want you, and now that I've met you in person, I'm even more convinced that you're the right person to work with."

Huh. This thug had an ambitious dream. Well, good for him. Strangely enough, it made me feel even worse about myself. This low-life, degenerate thug had more ambition than I did.

"OK, Briana, I know what you're thinking, and quit being so judgmental. Maybe I do what I do because unavoidable circumstances led me down the path that I was forced to take. Maybe I'm more than the rough exterior that you see. You know, I have a brain, and I also feel things just like everyone else."

Oh, brother. Was this really happening? I felt like it was a joke. How ridiculous. Yet I found myself admiring Rocco for having a dream. I wasn't qualified to help someone write a book, but I'm pretty sure that I wasn't dealing with the next Mordecai Richler either. Anyhow, I didn't really have a choice in the matter, did I?

"Rocco, I'll help you as much as I can with

your book. Once I've done that, Peter's debt will be paid, and you'll leave him alone. And one more thing, don't call me "honey" or "sweetheart" or any other words like that. OK?"

"OK, hon...*Briana*. We can start right away. I actually have an office not too far from where you live. We can work on the book at my office. "

He knows where I live. What else does he know about me? Well, for starters, he knew that I shopped at Costco. That's just great! As if I wasn't paranoid enough already. Another fine mess that I'm in due to Peter. I really should just let Rocco beat the shit right out of him!

"Look, I'll help you, but I still have my kids to take care of, and my home, and my job. So I can meet with you once a week. You can work on your book on your own, and when I meet with you, let's say on Friday afternoons, then I'll be able to help you work on whatever you came up with during the week."

So we agreed to meet on Friday afternoons at his office. He gave me his business card, and I was finally allowed to leave, with my *melted* ice cream and the rest of my groceries. Rocco had a business card! Can you believe it? The business card stated that he was a "Financial Consultant." That's pretty good! I was, however, surprised to learn that he was also a "Chartered Accountant." He did seem to be a little too smart to be just a simple "loan shark."

8

Frustrated in Montreal...

I never really had much sex in my life. Peter never seemed to be too interested in a lot of sex, at least with me. He could go for months without wanting to have sex with me, and when he would finally come to me, it wouldn't last very long. And believe me when I tell you that it was never about me. The foreplay was nonexistent, and once he would get what he wanted, he would be out of me and out of our bed. I always felt so sad afterwards, not to mention unsatisfied. It was like having one little potato chip. Sometimes a little itsy-bitsy taste is worse than having nothing at all. Of course, anytime that I had ever attempted to make a sexual move on Peter, he would tell me "later," or he would say that he needed to be up very early in the morning.

The worst was when I was pregnant. For some reason, I was so horny when I was pregnant, especially in my second trimester. I guess Peter was really turned off by my pregnant body. He really was not interested in me at all. One day I was preparing supper and a very long, hard cucumber began to look really good to me, if you know what I mean. That's when I told myself that I was going to get some action that night, even if it killed me. I showered, shaved, lathered myself in moisturizer, and wore the sexiest maternity clothing that I could find in my closet.

I practically ran to him when he came home from work that evening. "Supper is ready, but I want you to come sit with me on the sofa first." I reached out for Peter's hand and leaned forward a little, hoping that he would appreciate the sexy décolleté of my dress.

"Can't you give me some time to breathe, Briana! For God's sake..." Peter roughly broke away from my hand. The abruptness of his action made me realize just how desperately I was clutching on to him. He turned away from me and went into the kitchen. I was so hurt and embarrassed. I felt so fat and unattractive. I was pregnant and dying for some affection. I would've killed for a little sexual gratification. Peter looked so disgusted by me. I was disgusted with myself. I don't know why I thought that we could have had a normal married moment. Nothing about our relationship could ever have been considered normal. I was delusional to have thought otherwise.

9

Sexual Fantasies? Anyone...

I'm so pleased that I get to write about sexual fantasies It's such a learning experience for me. Since I don't get any real action in my life, well, the column allows me to live through other people's experiences. It turns out that some people really do have some wild fantasies. Personally, I don't think that I ever had too many sexual fantasies. I guess that's because I wasn't even getting the "basics" taken care of. I've always wanted to be hugged, caressed, kissed, and maybe a little "squeezed" here and there. The idea of "bondage love" never entered my mind. I gotta tell you, though, there's many a woman out there craving to be made love to while being held "captive." Maybe being "held captive" is really being "taken care of" by their lover. Many women are so used to being the caregivers in all of their relationships, so in their fantasies they want to finally be the ones to be taken care of. Maybe they are really looking for an outlet, to finally let go of all of the control and the stress and just let someone else do the thinking for once. Letting go of some of the responsibilities does sound good to me, but I still can't get comfortable with the idea of being held captive, with my wrists and legs bound, unable to move or get free. If anything, the idea simply stresses me out. But maybe you really can't knock it until you try it. Maybe with the right partner, I would try it.

One thing is for sure, and I've known this for a while: I have never really been properly "fucked" by a man. I've never experienced that mind-blowing, out-of-this-world feeling that some people describe when they talk about the sex that they've had. I've always felt a little empty after sex. I've felt a little lonely, disappointed, frustrated, and surely never satisfied. Writing my column has really shown me that I too want to rock somebody's world. More importantly, I now want someone to rock MY world. I think that I need to be loved. I want to be admired and I also want some affection in my life. However, I really long to be fucked the way that I was meant to be fucked. I crave it. Oh yeah, I want to make love, sure, who doesn't. But every now and then, a good hard fucking is really just what the doctor ordered. Sure, I'm a little horny and needy. But I'm so long overdue. Doesn't everyone deserve to get some mind-blowing sex at least once in their life before dying?

You know, there really isn't a shortage of fantasies to write about. My readers are encouraged to send in information about their fantasies. I then write a story involving a sexual fantasy using their information and ideas. I sometimes want to include one of the many personal fantasies that I now have, although my fantasies are very tame compared to some of the fantasies that some of my readers have.

I haven't seen my lover, Dr. Ferrante, in over forty-eight hours and I'm just dying to see him. He's been working so hard, saving lives. The latest life that he saved belongs to a woman in her twenties who had to have a lung transplant. My baby used his beautiful, strong, skilled hands to perform a miracle. After long, grueling hours in the operating room, he restores life, and the young woman can once again breathe easy. He's an angel. My angel.

The good doctor is so tired, but he feels a little restless. There's unfinished business for him to tend to. My business. Only I can give the doctor what he needs. His latest success makes him feel very alive, and wanting more. He longs to be rewarded by me for a job well done. He needs me. His hot, sexy man-

hood needs me.

He texts me: "I'll be there in twenty minutes. Take your clothes off. Leave your panties, bra, and high-heeled shoes on."

So the doctor is making a house call. I text back, "Keep your scrubs on." Dr. Ferrante is so hot in his scrubs. I hope he hasn't had a chance to shower. I love the way he smells and tastes after he's been operating all day. I imagine beads of perspiration trickling down his gorgeous chest and I'm so turned on by it. He's so virile.

He walks in and I can see that he's ready for me. He's got a big, beautiful bulge in his blue drawstring pants. He looks at me, through me, with deep longing and desire in his eyes. He's a sexual animal, and I'm his prey.

I stand in front of him, in my lacy pink briefs, and I can hardly speak because I'm so weak with wanting him. He takes my breath away. In a strained voice, I manage to ask him, "Difficult day, baby? Come to bed and let me make it all better for you." I need to fill my lungs with the hot, sexy scent of this hot, virile lung doctor. "Dr. Ferrante, tonight I will rock your world."

He sits on the edge of the bed, scrubs still on. I look down on him and whisper, "You work so hard to save so many lives, but now I will take you to places where you've never been before. Are you ready? Because I will take you out of this world."

As I begin to remove his pants, I look into his beautiful dark sexy eyes. "When you're at work, you belong to your patients who need you. But at night, you belong only to me."

I need him more than anyone else, even more than his patients.

"Only you can put out the fire inside of me. Breathe life into me. Come fill my lungs with your scent." And I take his beautiful manhood in my mouth completely, on bended knees.

I need to finish this if I want to include it in my column, and my fantasies are so tame compared to what comes in from my readers. Although I've imagined many different scenarios, I don't think that I'm quite ready to share any of them with my readers. How strange, it almost feels like I'd be kissing and telling. *Reality check, honey. Ain't nobody kissin' you, so there ain't nothin' to tell.* And I need to be careful because I do tend to have difficulty separating my reality from my dreams and fantasies.

My fantasies all involve Dr. Ferrante, and we always have wild, hot sex, anytime, anywhere. They are more of an erotic nature rather than pornographic. So you won't be hearing "bong chicka wawa" as the background music. I think that Marvin Gaye's "Sexual Healing" is probably more appropriate with us.

10

Operative Word of the Day: Flabbergasted

I was a little surprised to see how beautifully furnished Rocco's office is. It's so modern and expensive looking. It's decorated in black and white, with small pops of color. He must have an appreciation for art, because he has some beautiful paintings on his wall. I couldn't take my eyes off of a gorgeous painting in his waiting room. It's a Tamara de Lempicka. Does Rocco have any idea at all what a wonderful artist she is?

How strange it felt for me to see that Rocco and I have some things in common. We would both love to become writers, we both have an appreciation for art, and let's not forget that we would both love to see Peter's face bashed in by Rocco's fist! Ahhh, one can only dream.

I was a little taken aback by Rocco's assistant. Just where the fuck did he find this one? She is absolutely gorgeous! The woman has to be a model, because she looks like she belongs in a fashion magazine. She must be at least five foot nine, with long, blonde hair, a curvaceous and obviously fit figure, with a very nice rack indeed.

It all just left me a little speechless. By the look of things, it would appear to anyone that he is "legitimate." I just felt a little flabbergasted. I was expecting to help a Financial Consultant/Chartered Accountant/loan shark fulfill his dream of becoming a writer. Is it just me, or is this a little weird?

"Mrs. Rinaldi?" The gorgeous model/assistant's voice interrupted me from my daze. I had to close my mouth and wipe my lips with the back of my hand before I could turn to look at her and understand what she was saying. "Mr. Di Re will see you now. Please go right on in." I simply nodded my head and started to head for Rocco's office. Before going in, though, I turned to the model/assistant and said, "It's Briana, by the way." She looked at me with a smile. "OK, Briana." I couldn't help but wonder if Rocco is sleeping with the model/assistant. Of course they could actually be married to one another, but I just doubt it very much. I can see Rocco being someone's one night stand, but I just can't see him as anyone's husband.

Rocco was sitting at his desk and instantly got to his feet and came around to greet me with an outstretched hand. *Really?* He practically stalked me and cornered me in the Costco parking lot last week, but now he's all professional and offering me his hand. Oh boy, this is going to be interesting.

"It's so nice to see you again, Briana. Thank you for coming." *Like I had a choice.* "I thought we could work at my desk, but we could move to the sofa if you prefer. Whatever makes you feel comfortable. What can I get you to drink? Coffee? Soft drink? Maybe something to eat?"

"No, thank you. I'm good." Then Rocco looked at me, in silence, for what seemed like a few minutes. He had an almost regretful expression on his face.

"Briana, I know that you don't think too highly of me and you don't really want to be here right now. I feel badly about the whole situation with Peter, and especially how I got you to agree to this. But I just know that you are the right person to help me out. Please, you agreed to do this for me, so try to be a little more positive about it. It will make things so much more enjoyable for the both of us."

I took in what Rocco had said to me. He sounded so sincere, so positive and excited. I also took the time to look at his office. It's even more beautifully furnished than his waiting room. Very clean, modern, expensive looking. His desk is very big and the top of it is made out of glass. I couldn't help but wonder if he and the model/assistant had sex on his desk, or maybe they made themselves a little more comfortable on his big, soft black leather sofa. *Fuck me!* Why was I thinking of such disgusting things that were none of my business?

"Sure, Rocco. I'm here and I will help you as much as I can. But don't forget that I don't have any experience at all with writing a book." I moved past Rocco and made myself comfortable on a chair by his desk.

When I went to sit down, I noticed that on the wall behind my chair and facing Rocco's was a cluster of many photographs of a woman. At first I thought that it was a whole bunch of different women, but as I looked more closely I noticed that the photographs were all of the same woman. There were photos of her laughing, sleeping, smiling, being serious, looking straight at the camera, looking off somewhere. And then I noticed that there was also a framed photo of the same woman on Rocco's desk. Who is this woman that Rocco is obviously obsessed with? Should "stalker" be added to his business card? I wanted to ask him who she was, but I didn't feel that I should. It's probably best to simply do what I agreed to do, and keep things strictly business.

"OK, Rocco. Show me what you've got."

I was once again a little flabbergasted by Rocco. His writing is actually quite good. He has some pretty interesting ideas. He strikes me as having a lot of experience in the world, so maybe this is what makes him interesting. He just needs help putting his ideas and thoughts into words and on paper. We got an awful lot done, but after a few hours of working with him, I had to go pick up Marco and Elisa.

As I was about to leave, I just couldn't help myself. "Rocco, who's the woman in the pictures?" He looked a little surprised by my question, and I thought that I saw sadness in his eyes before he looked away from me. "She's my wife."

"Oh, you're married. She's beautiful." I was being sincere; she was beautiful. Not in a glamorous way, but in a more pure, wholesome way. She had long, dark, curly hair, with big dark eyes, a small nose, and full, pouty lips. She seemed to have a petite frame, and she had a pale complexion. She just looked too nice to be married to a loan shark.

"Yes, she is beautiful. Was beautiful."

I didn't say anything. I just stood in front of Rocco and couldn't look away. Maybe it's because I was pre-menstrual and feeling a little emotional, but I instantly felt a lump in my throat and I could feel my eyes beginning to sting with suppressed tears. I immediately knew what Rocco was saying, of course.

He was shuffling some papers on his desk, pretending to be interested in what was written on them. "She died about three years ago. She suffered a heart attack after having a double lung transplant."

He quickly looked up at me and did a double take as he noticed the tears beginning to swell up in my eyes. "OK, Briana. Time for you to go now. I'll see you next week."

I stood there for another minute or so, unable to move for some reason. "Briana, go now. Your kids are waiting for you."

I just turned and slowly headed for the door. I barely managed to quietly let out an "I'm sorry," unable to actually face Rocco as I said it. I just felt so bad for him. He obviously loved this woman. And he obviously still felt pain at the simple mention of his wife.

Yeah, I'd say "flabbergasted" was the operative word of the day.

11

The Gangsta with a Heart

I have been working with Rocco for weeks now, and to my great surprise, I am actually enjoying myself. Rocco is a very complex person, and there is certainly more than meets the eye with this guy. I actually don't mean this in a negative way. I know that Rocco has a dark side to him, although I don't know the extent of his darkness. But I am also learning that he has a totally different side to him. Rocco is a gentleman. He is a little "old school" in so many ways. I would say that he must be about forty years old, but his behavior sometimes makes him seem like he belongs in a time when men were the "breadwinners" who just took care of everything. The feminist in me cringes, but the single mom, the tired, over-worked, and over-stressed woman in me, longs to be "taken care of" by a strong, responsible man. Rocco is the type to open the door for you. He always asks me how I'm doing and how my kids are, and he sounds so sincere, like he actually wants to know. He always seems genuinely concerned about me. He has a quiet strength about him, and he is so tall, dark, and, yes, handsome. As strange as this may sound, I feel good when I'm with him. As dangerous as I'm sure he must really be, I feel safe with Rocco. I'm a little embarrassed to admit that I often feel a little frightened in the evenings when I'm alone at home. I think that I take a little bit of that fear with me wherever I go. And yet, with Rocco, I never feel afraid. We have quickly become friends, and it just feels natural. I know that Rocco would never do anything to hurt me, and he would actually do whatever necessary to protect me. I just know this in my gut, and I really appreciate it.

Rocco and I were in his office, working on his book. He was rubbing the scar above his left eye with his thumb. I quickly learned that he does this when he's in deep thought. His book is about a wealthy Montreal Italian family that owns several businesses. The family is very well known, as they own several companies, hotels, and even a sports team. They are very much in the public eye, and they never miss an opportunity to attend charitable events where they get to show the public how supposedly great, giving, and wonderful they are. The reality, of course, is that they are really a very dark family, with a dark past. Any charity that this family supports, or any other good cause that they back, is really just an attempt to restore their dark reputation that keeps coming up every now and then in the media. The reality is that they are narcissistic, hypocritical, self-serving, and very dangerous indeed. Rocco assures me that his book is fiction, or at least it will be marketed as such.

You know, we all look down on the "obvious" bad guys. But what about those who pretend to be moral, ethical, charitable members of society, who have created, *bought and paid for*, a perfect image for themselves. Their true nature is very different indeed. What I can't stand about the family that Rocco is writing about is how greedy and selfish they are. Ask any Italian in Montreal about this particular family, and I guarantee that everyone knows of a personal story, either directly or indirectly, detailing an incident that shows how corrupt they really are. They have so much money, and yet they just can't stand to see others attain financial success. So many struggling Italians have stories about how this particular family sabotaged small businesses in and around Montreal with their threats. It makes my blood boil just thinking about it!

However, it turns out that Rocco was in a very

pensive mood for reasons other than his book.

"Rocco, what's going on with you today? You don't seem to be that interested in your book. What is it?"

"I just have a lot on my mind, that's all. Sorry for taking up so much of your time, Briana. It must feel like such a waste of time for you being here when I'm like this?"

"No, of course not, Rocco. I already told you that I like working with you on your book. It's fun for me. It's just really obvious that something is troubling you and, you know, well, you can talk to me if you like."

Rocco just looked at me for a few moments, and I felt like I could actually see what he was thinking. He was considering if he should open up to me or not.

"Briana, I believe that I already told you that my wife had a double lung transplant about three years ago. After Angela died, I had a hard time letting go. I eventually figured out that the best way to keep her with me, always, was to do what I do best, and that's make a lot of money. So I raised a lot of money to help people with lung diseases get the help that they need to live a long, normal life. Angela would've loved that because she was always involved in some type of project or another to raise money or awareness for a cause."

"Rocco, I haven't known you that long, *but I gotta tell ya*, you are quickly becoming one of the most interesting people that I have ever met!"

He obviously liked hearing this. He just looked down at his pants and with his hand brushed off some lint that wasn't even there, but I could see that he had a smile on his face.

"So, what exactly are you doing? How much money are we talking about? Who are you helping? Is it just in the area of lung transplantation or lung disease in general?"

Rocco looked a little amused, wide-eyed, and he had a little smirk on his face. With both hands raised in front of him, he looked at me and said, "Take it easy, honey. Why are you so excited over this? It's no big deal, you know. It's just business for me, that's all."

"Oh, come on, Rocco. You're so full of it. We both know that it's not just business for you. You don't need to pretend with me, not anymore. I think I already know you well enough to fully understand that you aren't the big bad wolf, even though that's what you want everyone to think. It's just so beautiful that you would help so many people in the name of love. It's so romantic, and—"

Rocco then cut me off and a bewildered look replaced the amusement that I had seen in his eyes. "Enough now, Briana. Don't make this into something that it isn't. And don't for one minute think that I'm not the *big bad wolf*, because men like me eat little girls like you for breakfast."

"First of all, Rocco, don't speak to me like I'm a stupid little girl. I'm not much younger than you are." And then I just stood there, angry but not completely angry. Rocco had not managed to suck all of the joy out of me, and I realized that he was condescending and insulting because he didn't want me to see his sensitive, more vulnerable side. After a few moments of silence, Rocco looked at me with an expression that was a cross between amusement and impatience.

"And second of all? Briana?"

"There is no second of all. I just think that it's great that you thought to do something so honorable. My mom was diagnosed with lung cancer over a year ago, and there isn't a day that goes by that I don't wish that I could do something, anything, to make a difference in the world. You know, lung cancer needs research funding drastically. I really feel that I need to do something to help raise awareness for this type of cancer. Rocco, I just really admire you for doing something that will make a difference."

"I'm not as honorable as you think I am. My shrink gave me the idea to do this, and making money just comes naturally to me. So I figured, why not, I'll try it out. And Briana, I will admit that doing this makes me feel like Angela is still here with me, in my heart, because I know that this would make her very happy."

Oh my God, this big brute of a man with unruly dark hair and scars and all, albeit in an Armani suit, is such a sweetheart. He is beautiful. *Ah, NO, I'm not falling for him, really.* It's not like that. I have fallen for him as a friend, though. My heart still belongs to another, even though he will never belong to me.

"I created the Angel's Breath Research Foundation about two and a half years ago. It was created in honor of Angela, and the funds raised are mainly for research to improve the outcomes of lung transplant surgery."

"Are you having issues with your foundation? Is that why you looked so pensive, and troubled?"

"I'm not troubled, exactly but I am a little irritated. We're having an event next Saturday night, and I'm always expected to attend these things. You know, I'm happy raising the money for the Foundation, but I just hate these public events that I have to attend. I'm more of a behind the scenes kind of guy."

"I get that you appreciate your privacy, but maybe you should get over this adversity to public events. I mean, really, you belong out there, in the public eye. You are a money-maker! You are well spoken, you're smart, sociable, you're not bad looking, and your story is so touching and beautiful. Love and romance just warm people's hearts, and open up their wallets."

"I'm not interested in warming people's hearts with my story, Briana. Next weekend is the Grand Prix weekend here in Montreal. Some of the wealthiest people in the world will be in town, mainly because they have tickets for the race. The timing of this event is perfect, because the entire trip for these people is really all about having a great time and spending big money. It's the time for these bigwigs to show off a little and flaunt how much cash they really have."

"Sounds right up your alley, Rocco. So what's the problem?"

"It's really *not* up my alley. Like I said, I prefer to be behind the scenes. The event will take place at the Old Port in Montreal, on a luxury yacht that I chartered. The event is set up as a type of "whodunit" murder mystery live experience. The guests will be provided with cards that will reveal to them the role that they will have to play. There will be a lot of drinking, of course, and things could get a little intense. Once the yacht sets sail, the guests will not be able to disembark for several hours. I'm just not looking forward to being stuck at the event for so long. Making small talk with a bunch of rich but essentially boring people for so long is just too much for me to bear. OK, Briana, don't look so awestruck. It's really not a good time."

"Look, it's just something that you need to do to help raise more money for your research foundation. Just keep telling yourself that. So, who will accompany you to this grand event?" I just couldn't miss the opportunity to try and find out if he's seeing anyone special. I know that he must be seeing someone, because he's too good-looking not to. He's not cutesy, but very manly, and I can see how a lot of women would appreciate that. Maybe he would take his model/assistant with him. By the way, her name is Vanessa. Even her name sounds a little sexy to me.

"Why, Briana, are you fishing for an invitation to the event?"

Rocco began to rub the scar above his left eye with his thumb, and I knew that I was in trouble. Just what was he thinking about? One thing was for sure: it involved me and it wasn't good.

"Oh, don't be ridiculous, Rocco. I have no desire to go to your little event." I was actually very intrigued. I was dying to go to this type of event. It sounded like it would be so much fun, but I would never admit it to Rocco. "I was just a little curious to know if you are seeing anyone. Are you going with Vanessa? Maybe it's none of my business, but aren't we friends now? It's OK for friends to ask inappropriate questions, right?"

"You're right, it is none of your business if I'm seeing anyone, and yes, I think we are friends now." He had such a way of speaking down to you when he wanted to. So condescending and embarrassing.

"OK, Briana, you will accompany me to this event." He then stopped rubbing his scar and walked over to the wet bar in his office.

"Ah, Rocco, have you lost your marbles? I wasn't fishing for an invitation, and I certainly don't want to be your *date* to this thing!"

"Come on now, Briana, we both know that you'd get a kick out of it, and as you said, we're friends now. So can't you accompany me as a friend? I'd rather go with you than with anyone else." He poured himself a drink, his typical Johnnie Walker Blue Label. He poured another and brought it over to me. *Like I drink whisky!*

"Rocco, why would you rather go with me? Why wouldn't you rather go with someone that you are, um, romantically involved with?"

"Sweetheart, I'm not *romantically involved* with anyone. I'm a man, so yes, I have my needs filled by a lot of women. But there isn't one special woman for me, not anymore. And I won't complicate things by bringing one of my women to an event. I like women to know exactly where I stand with them, and I don't believe in misleading anyone. And my work is too important to me to expose it to anyone that I don't really care about. With you, Briana, there aren't any expectations. We're friends, and I'll have someone that I enjoy talking to with me for the long, boring evening."

Well, he was honest, and I appreciated it. I really did want to go, but my pride was stopping me from jumping up and down.

"Briana, there's no need for pride amongst friends." And he's so perceptive.

Oh, what the hell! If he could be honest, then so could I. "OK, sure, I'll go with you. It'll be fun."

"Good. It's a date! Now, are you still up to doing a little bit of work, or are you just too excited about next week to get anything done?"

I gave him my "fuck off" look, took a sip of my drink, and got back to work.

The event is on a Saturday night, on the

weekend of the Grand Prix, which marks the official, unofficial start of the fabulous summer festival season in Montreal.

12

The Main Event

I had a hard time finding something appropriate to wear to the event, mainly because I've become so insecure about my looks. I work really hard, and I'm just too busy or too exhausted to spend any real time on myself. But I did take a little bit of time, and I found a really beautiful dress.

I chose a dark, sand-colored, sequined bandage-knit dress. There are solid knit straps that scoop on the bodice to frame the bust and create a straight neckline. It has an open back, it is formfitting, and the pencil skirt hits just above the knee. It's so beautiful, and I just love it. It is sparkly yet classy, and trendy enough to make me look like I could not only fit in to a cool event, but I could even stand out. And the shoes are simple. Simply gorgeous! They are sand-colored just like the straps on the dress, open toe, ankle wrap, and a four-and-a-quarter-inch heel. I felt a little guilty spending so much money on myself, but I hadn't done this in so long, so I just went ahead and bought it all.

On the day of the event, I had my nails and my hair done. I had my hair cut shorter than usual, and it was liberating! I guess getting rid of something old and embracing something new felt cathartic somehow. I felt empowered! My kids were spending the day and evening with my mom at her home. Rocco insisted on picking me up at my home so we could go to the event together. We didn't have our weekly work session this week because Rocco was too busy. I was a little relieved; I was just too anxious to get any real work done.

Rocco was at my door by 6 p.m. Cocktails were at 6:30 p.m., and dinner at 7:30 p.m. I gave myself one last look in the mirror before getting to the door. "Hi, Rocco. Do you want to come in, or should we just go?"

Rocco looked a little surprised, and he hesitated before responding. "We should go. It's getting late, and I need to be there on time." He looked really good. He was in a slim-fit, charcoal-colored suit and light-blue shirt. No tie. The color of his shirt really made his eyes stand out. They looked so light against the darkness of his skin, his longish, dark, wavy hair, and his dark, expen-

sive-looking suit. So as I was walking alongside
Rocco to his car that was parked in my driveway, I
couldn't help but feel a little disappointed that he
didn't comment on how I looked. Always the gentleman, he opened the car door for me. Through a
crooked smile, he finally gave me what I craved.
"You look gorgeous, Briana." And then he ruined
it for me! "And I'm not too happy about this." He
made his way to the driver's side of the car and
slid his long frame behind the wheel of his black
Mercedes-Benz.

I was a little confused by his comment. "Am I
not dressed appropriately for this evening? What
aren't you happy about?"

"You look beautiful, Briana. The problem is,
you're not going to blend in. You are going to stand
out for sure in that dress. What the hell, Briana. I
told you that I prefer to stay behind the scenes. But
if I walk in with you on my arm, well, there's just
going to be a lot of gossip, that's all."

It felt good to be told that I looked nice, but
Rocco's compliments sounded more like an accu-
sation, and his words were hurtful. No man had
told me that I looked good in such a long time, so
I was really craving some attention. I had spent
too much money to let the night be ruined by some
stupid, insensitive words. So I swallowed back my
tears, turned to Rocco, and with a shaky voice told
him how I felt.

"Rocco, how dare you speak to me in this way?
I put a lot of effort into tonight, as a favor to you,

and you insult me and hurt my feelings. I'm not your date, remember? We're just going as friends, and friends walk in together, but not arm in arm. As far as anyone is concerned tonight, I am just another guest at this party. I'm not your date, OK! And it's not too late to turn back the car and take me home. If you prefer, I don't have to go tonight at all. No big deal to me!" Actually, it was a big deal to me.

Rocco looked a little shocked. "Briana, I'm so sorry. Forgive me."

We drove the rest of the way in silence. When we got there, Rocco came over to my side and opened the door for me. He held out his hand and once I was out of the car, he slipped my arm in the crook of his arm. He looked at me with a crooked grin. "Ah, what the hell, we are going to be the best-looking couple in the place!"

There were over five hundred guests! Rocco explained that only thirty of the guests would have the privilege of sitting at the "murder mystery" dinner table. These guests paid a lot of money to sit at the most popular table. I couldn't help myself from thinking about how many debts I could pay off with the amount of what one ticket cost. The difference between my life and some of these peo-ple's lives couldn't be more obvious.

The yacht was beautiful, and everyone looked so amazing. It was like a scene out of a movie. I noticed several people checking me out, and it just felt so good. Rocco was busy tending to his responsibilities, shaking hands with everyone and welcoming them onboard. I was having a cocktail, a green apple martini, and I was completely awe-struck with everything and everyone.

And then *he* walked into the room.

I noticed him immediately. Dr. Alex Ferrante had just walked into the dining room, with a gorgeous tall blonde on his arm. It was like he sensed my presence too, because he turned his head in my direction. Our eyes locked instantly. I couldn't believe that my love, my angel, was here. And just who the hell was that Amazon on his arm, oozing sexuality?

"Briana, are you OK? Why do you look like you're about to go into cardiac arrest?" I hadn't noticed Rocco make his way toward me, but he was now standing in front of me, blocking the good doctor from my view.

"Rocco, I'm fine." I kept shifting my position so that I could face Dr. Ferrante, but Rocco kept shifting his position along with me, so that he kept on blocking my view. He was really getting on my nerves tonight. "OK, Rocco, what are you doing? Why are you *in my face?*"

"What are you talking about? How many drinks have you had?" With a crooked grin, he pointed his finger at me, like he was scolding an insolent child. "No more drinks before you eat, got it? *Lightweight!*" Oh yeah, Rocco was really getting on my last nerve tonight.

And then Dr. Ferrante was directly behind

Rocco. "Hey, Rocco, how are you?" Rocco turned around and instantly grabbed the doctor and gave him a quick *man hug*. You know, the type of hug that's really just an arm hug, with *no full-body contact.*

"Hey, Alex. It's so good to see you. Hi, Felicia, you're looking gorgeous as usual."

So, her name is Felicia. I guess Rocco didn't have any issues telling this woman how gorgeous she looked.

Rocco turned to me and grabbed my hand. "This is Briana Rinaldi. She is a friend of mine, and she's also working with me on a business project. Briana, this is--"

I interrupted him and finished his sentence. "Dr. Ferrante, good evening." The doctor and I exchanged hellos, and he smiled at me. The tall blonde and I also exchanged pleasantries. *Biotch.* Dr. Ferrante looked at me with that deep, penetrating look of his, and it didn't take long for me to realize that he still had that same old effect on me. I felt like I could hardly breathe, and I just couldn't take my eyes off of him. I was thirsty, and he was an icy cold drink.

"Oh, you know each other." Rocco finally let go of my hand, and he turned to me with a questioning look on his face."

"Rocco, Dr. Ferrante operated on my mom when she had lung cancer. He's her surgeon."

"Oh, is that right? Dr. Ferrante was also Angela's doctor. He's also the President of the

Angel's Breath Research Foundation. Alex and I go back a long way, and we're very good friends."

And then the blonde, *Felicia,* reached for Rocco's arm and told him that she had the role cards for the murder mystery participants but that she needed him to help her distribute them. Apparently, this Felicia babe actually works for Dr. Ferrante and Rocco at the Foundation, as the secretary. So it seems that Rocco likes his secretaries to be blonde and gorgeous.

"Alex, Briana, please excuse us."

The doctor and I simultaneously said, "Of course. Go ahead." Dr. Ferrante and I looked at each other and laughed. And then we were alone.

"You stopped coming by with your mom to her appointments. Why is that, Briana?"

Thank goodness for that apple martini, because it gave me the courage to not only face Dr. Ferrante, but actually speak to him too. Good God, Rocco is right, I am a lightweight.

"I stopped coming by because, in case you hadn't noticed, *and I really do hope that you forgot,* I had a hard time controlling myself around you. So I figured, in an effort to avoid embarrassing myself anymore, that I should just stay away. And I really don't want my behavior to reflect poorly on my mom. She still needs you to be her doctor." There, I said it. Good for me! For months I had imagined myself saying that to him.

Dr. Ferrante just looked at me, expressionless, and he took his time to speak. "I'm your mother's doctor, and your *behavior* won't change that. Don't feel like you need to stay away. Really, don't worry about it." Wasn't he impressed by how brave I was, being that direct and all? *Obviously not.*

He then looked at me, slowly, up and down. He had a look of appreciation on his face. Was I imagining this again? But I felt different this time. Oh, he still made me weak in the knees, but I also knew that I looked good, so I felt more confident. While he was looking at me, I hungrily stared back at him and felt my knees weaken again. He is just so fuckin' hot. His slim-fit dark suit jacket hugged his shoulders and really emphasized his broad frame. He looked so manly.

"You look very nice, Briana."

"Thanks. So do you." I didn't tell him that I wanted to tear his clothes off, throw myself on him, and have my way with him.

Rocco had come back, and he was oblivious to the hot chemistry that was so obviously brewing between me and the good doctor. "OK, Briana. They will begin to serve dinner now, so come along. Alex, you're seated at my table. Are you ready to eat now, or are you still working the room?"

"Go ahead. I'll be there in a little while." So Rocco and I made our way to our table. Hearing Rocco speak to Dr. Ferrante in such a familiar way, using his first name, made me think about the last text that I had sent him. I had been familiar with him too, calling him Alex, but he didn't like it coming from me. I still feel so embarrassed by what I wrote, and it's funny how when I think about him now, even just in my thoughts, I can't really use his first name because I feel like I can't be that familiar with him. You know, to be fair, he should really call me Mrs. Rinaldi. Why does he get to call me by my first name?

The meal was delicious. I would've loved seconds of everything, but my dress was so snug, and I couldn't risk any bulges getting loose. I was seated next to Rocco at a table with ten other people. The doctor, *Alex*, was seated next to Felicia. I have to say, they really looked good together. What a striking couple they made. He is so dark and handsome, and she is so *BLONDE* and beautiful! I noticed that when she spoke to him, she placed her mouth so close to his ear, and she kept it there long after she finished saying what she had to say to him. And it's not like it was so loud in the room that she couldn't just speak to him from a regular distance, like normal human beings. Oh, they were flirting with each other, alright.

"Are you done glaring at them? What is your problem, anyways?" Rocco leaned over and asked me in a very low tone so as not to let anyone hear our conversation.

"What? Who? I'm not glaring at anyone. But don't you think that those two are getting a little too cozy for this table? I'm about to toss my filet mignon. And correct me if I'm wrong, but isn't he a married man?"

Rocco laughed at my comments. "You are

such a prude! And, by the way, you are wrong. Alex isn't married." I wanted Rocco to elaborate, but I didn't get the chance to ask him because he was needed in the murder mystery room. I couldn't sit there any longer, by myself, and watch the man that I had obsessed with for so long flirt shamelessly with another woman. So I got up and went out on deck for some fresh air. I was having trouble breathing inside. I was jealous, and it was hurtful seeing him with someone else. I was leaning on the railing and wishing that the evening would just come to an end already.

"Don't do it. Don't jump! The water is way too cold." Dr. Ferrante had come up behind me, and I was practically in his arms when I turned to face him. The look in his eyes took my breath away. He flashed that lazy, sexy smile of his, and my eyes simply fixated on his mouth. I wanted to kiss it. Taking my hand, he rubbed the inside of my wrist with his thumb. What was he doing to me? "Briana, why did you leave the table? Why are you outside?"

"I just needed some air."

"You looked a little upset. Are you upset with me, Briana? Did I do something to offend you?"

"Of course not. Why would you think that?" I felt like I was beginning to panic. Was I that obvious? Did everyone else at the table notice it too? And then his fingers tightened a little on my wrist.

"I can feel your pulse rate. You need to take it easy, or before we know it I'll have to give you mouth-to-mouth." And that smile of his, together with being so close to him and feeling his touch, well, it was just too much for me.

"What are you doing, Dr. Ferrante?"

He smiled and said, "Alex."

"*What are you doing, Dr. Ferrante?*" This time I said it slowly, for emphasis. I felt like I had been down this road before with him, well, somewhat. I wasn't about to play this game with him only to look like a fool once he decided that play time was over.

"What did you really mean by sending me that last text of yours, Briana?"

"Look, Dr. Ferrante, it was very silly and inappropriate of me to send you that text. I didn't mean any disrespect, and I really didn't want to offend you."

"You didn't offend me in the least. But why did you just stop texting me, or coming by with your mom to her visits?"

"Oh, come on now. You were obviously upset by my text. Your response could not have been clearer."

"I wouldn't say that I was upset over your text. I remember being upset, but only because I had a very difficult surgery that day that didn't go as I had planned."

"Briana, here you are." Boy, that Rocco sure had a way of popping up at the wrong time. Although the doctor let go of my wrist when Rocco arrived, his eyes never let go of mine.

"Am I interrupting anything?" Rocco just looked at me, and at Alex, and he obviously felt the tension between us.

"No. I was just asking Dr. Ferrante about his work with the Angel's Breath Research Foundation. It's admirable how much work he puts into it, considering what a busy doctor he is and how in demand his services are." Dr. Ferrante just looked at me with a half grin on his face and his left eyebrow slightly raised. I felt a little pleased with myself, and that should have tipped me off that there was trouble ahead because I never have the upper hand in anything.

"Briana, you really have no idea how lucky we are that Alex is working on the Foundation. You're right, he is very busy and much in demand. And still, he takes the time to help us out." Rocco patted Dr. Ferrante on the shoulder when he said this, and I could really see genuine admiration in Rocco's eyes for Alex.

"OK, knock it off now." Alex was flashing that sexy smile of his. *You know, the one that makes me want to tear off his clothes.* "But we really could use some help with the Foundation. It requires a lot of time that I just don't have. If we expand and increase any funding activity, then we really need to get some help." Both Rocco and Alex were looking at me. Rocco was rubbing his scar, while Alex had a sly look on his face. And I knew then that I was done feeling pleased with myself.

"Alex, you know Briana here has been helping

me with a personal project of mine, and she's really a godsend. She's just so helpful, and really a pleasure to have around."

"I can see how it must be a great pleasure for you to have her around." The doctor's eyes gleamed, and he actually looked like a mischievous little boy who was up to no good.

"Briana, didn't you once say to me that you would love to make a difference in the world, and that lung cancer is seriously lacking awareness and funding? I would love for you to get involved in our foundation. I know that you would really be a great help to us, and seriously, I can't tell you how satisfying it is to feel that you're doing something good to help so many in need."

Damn that Rocco! Sure, I wanted to do something honorable and selfless. But I'm also a single mom, and I have to work for a living, and I'm already helping Rocco write his damn book! But of course, he now put me in a situation where I would look so selfish and uncharitable if I didn't get involved with this foundation.

"I'm sorry, Briana, for asking this of you. It's too much, and I realize that." Rocco turned to Alex while reaching for my hand. "Briana here has two gorgeous kids, and she works a hell of a lot. She doesn't have the time for this, and it wasn't fair of me to ask her."

And now I just looked so foolish. Yeah, sure I'm busy, but certainly not busier than Dr. Ferrante, and *he* takes the time to do charity work.

"No, please, Rocco, don't be silly. I would love to help out, but from my understanding, your foundation supports mainly lung transplants. While I think that your work is great, I do want to devote some time to charity, but I really had my heart set on helping out specifically with lung cancer."

"OK, Briana. I want to help you out with this." Rocco took both of my hands in his and squeezed a little. "Briana, we are expanding at the Foundation, and I would love for our foundation to focus on increasing awareness and funding for lung cancer. You can take care of this new objective." Rocco looked so pleased, almost emotional. What could I do, or say for that matter?

"It sounds great. I'm looking forward to it." I really did want to help out, and it was wonderful that Rocco was providing this great opportunity. But I just felt so overwhelmed.

Rocco hugged me, and so did Dr. Ferrante. It felt like the doctor's hug lasted a little bit longer than normal. "Welcome to the Foundation, Briana. I think I'm going to like working with you."

"Oh, you bet you will, Alex. She's a real gem, this one."

"Briana, we'll work out the details next week. Now, let's get back inside. There's a chocolate cake in there with my name on it! And Alex, you better get back to Felicia before she sinks her claws into an unsuspecting innocent who won't be able to handle her womanly charms as easily as you can."

"You're right, Rocco." The doctor chuckled

and followed us back inside. "I hope that I'm not too late."

As if on cue, the gorgeous blonde was the first person we bumped into as we went back inside. She smiled radiantly up at the doctor and grabbed his arm. She then pouted her lips in an exaggerated way and batted her long, false eyelashes at him. "Alex, where have you been? I've been so lonely without you. Come dance with me." And with that, the doctor smiled down at her and led her to the dance floor.

Absolutely shameless. They danced so well together. What a striking couple they made. I felt so jealous, angry, stupid and hurt. I can't blame him for liking beautiful, sexy women. *Oh, why can't he like average, pathetic, loser types?*

And as Felicia moved her curvaceous body into Alex's, to the sultry rhythm of the music, I dug my fork into an absolutely delicious chocolate cake. For the first time in my life, chocolate did not fulfill any of my needs.

I turned to Rocco, who appeared to really be enjoying a second piece of cake, and I knew that this was a good time to ask and possibly get some personal information about Dr. Ferrante.

"OK, Rocco. Spill. What's the story with Dr. Ferrante? Last I heard, he was a married man."

"Briana, like to gossip much?" Rocco looked at me with that crooked grin of his. "Just kidding, honey. I know that you're a good girl."

Rocco practically inhaled the last chunk of

chocolate cake on his plate. He took a sip of his espresso and leaned back on his chair as if he was getting ready to tell me a story that I would not believe.

"Alex was indeed married, but that was a long time ago. His marriage ended because his wife had a difficult time being monogamous. He actually caught her in bed with another man. His wife brought this guy to their home, in their bed. And apparently this guy was a stranger that she met earlier that day at the mall. Alex later learned that his wife had done this on many occasions. She pled not guilty on the grounds of being a sex addict."

"Rocco, are you kidding me? Who the heck did he marry?"

"*Ah wait*, Briana, there's more. They got divorced. Look, I'm only telling you this because you're going to be working with him, and I want you to understand where he's coming from if you see things that you may not approve of. He's a stand-up guy, in every way, and you'll soon come to learn this."

"What will I *see* that I won't approve of, Rocco?"

"Don't look like that, Briana! It's just, well, you can be a little bit of a prude, you know."

"Me? A prude? That's just crazy talk. Did you forget that I write about *sexual fantasies* for a living?"

"OK, honey, just because you write about them doesn't mean that you know anything about them."

"Rocco, you are getting dangerously close...to getting *me*...to tell *you*...to *fuck off.*"

"A foul-mouthed prude!"

"Just please finish telling your story." I wanted to get up and leave because I was so offended by Rocco's words. But I just sat there, eagerly waiting for the brute to continue on with his story. I had to find out more about what happened with Alex.

"As you can see, Alex is a pretty good-looking guy. A lot of women appreciate his good looks, and, well, Alex appreciates what women so eagerly offer him. You can't blame the guy. In fact, he's always honest with women. They know not to expect any commitment from him, and they know where they stand with him. So you might see him with a lot of different women. No big deal, OK?"

"Sure, no big deal." I didn't want to see him with a lot of women. Just seeing him with that *Felicia* babe was more than I could handle. How could I work with Alex? I was setting myself up for more pain. I just want to be happy. No more pain. "You said there was more?"

"Oh yeah, there's more. A couple of years after the divorce, Alex's ex-wife got sick. She was diagnosed with schizophrenia. She just got worse as time went by, and the medication did nothing to help her. Finally, one day, she just stopped talking. She was unresponsive, in a daze. She's been in a catatonic state ever since, and it's been years now."

I couldn't believe what he was telling me. "How did Alex handle it?"

"Alex was the only person that gave a damn about her. He got her the best care that money could buy. Not even her family stepped in to help out. You know, they were divorced, but Alex still felt obligated to take care of his ex-wife. He couldn't stand the thought of leaving her in a psychiatric hospital, all alone, with nobody to really care for her. She lives in a condo that he bought for her, and she's got round-the-clock medical care. So when I say that he's a stand-up guy, it's not just because he's a respected surgeon who saves lives on a daily basis."

Wow, it *was* a story that was hard to believe. I already knew that Alex was a good person. I mean, wasn't that part of why and how I fell for him? But this was huge. Is he still in love with his ex-wife? Maybe he is, and that's why he continues to take care of her.

"Rocco, is Dr. Ferrante in love with his wife?"

"He cares about what happens to her, and he's a very loyal person. But he did divorce her. And anytime anyone refers to her as his wife, he immediately corrects them and calls her his ex-wife. So I don't think that he's *in love* with her, no."

Rocco and I were so engrossed in our conversation so we didn't even notice when Alex and Felicia made their way back to the table. "Rocco, I'm going to call it a night. Early morning tomorrow," Alex said.

I hadn't even noticed that the yacht had returned to the port and was docked.

"Are you working tomorrow, Alex?"

"No, I actually have an early morning tee time."

"Oh, Alex, wouldn't you rather sleep in tomorrow?" Felicia sexily slurred her question as she snuggled her nose in his neck. And I thought that I was going to be sick for sure.

I looked over at Rocco, who had that crooked grin on his face and nodded his head as if to say, *you do know what she's really asking him.*

"I would like to sleep in, Felicia, but you know there's not much that I would rather do than play golf. So an early night is what I need."

Yes! You tell her, Alex!

Felicia stroked the doctor's hair with her hand and said, "I need one too, Alex."

And that was just too much for me. "Rocco, I think that I should be going too."

"Sure, hon, let's go."

We all made our way off the yacht. We exchanged goodbyes, and before I knew it I was back in Rocco's gorgeous little car, on my way back home. Well, the evening wasn't exactly what I had expected, but it sure was eventful.

I met the object of all of my fantasies, learned a whole lot more about him, and got myself involved in more work that I know nothing about and that I'm not qualified to do. On the other hand, I didn't even participate in the murder mystery as I had hoped to.

When we got to my house, Rocco got out of

his car and walked me to my front door. "Rocco, I'd invite you in, but I'm too tired and I just really want to get to sleep."

"Of course. Listen, thank you for tonight. And thank you for everything, Briana. I really appreciate all of your help, with tonight, with my book, with everything. You're a good friend, and you know that if you ever need anything, you can count on me."

"I know, Rocco. Thanks." And I really did know that I had met a true, loyal friend in Rocco. "Good night, Rocco. I'll see you next week. And thank you too, for tonight."

I was truly drained. I got undressed, slipped into comfortable pajamas and brushed my teeth. I got into bed and just felt so alone. I had been foolish. It hurt me to see Dr. Ferrante be so intimate with another woman. I learned a little too much about him that evening. I felt like crying, but I couldn't. I was empty. If I was going to begin working at the Foundation, then I would surely see Alex on a somewhat regular basis. I'm not sure that I was strong enough for that.

I missed my kids, but it was probably a good thing that they were spending the night at my mom's. And I really needed to sleep, so I decided that my worries would have to wait until morning. I would just have to figure things out in the morning. Everything is always clearer in daylight.

13

Wet and Delicious

"Is Dr. Ferrante still in surgery?" I asked a nurse.

"No, he's all done. He's just getting changed and will be here shortly. Do you have an appointment? Are you a patient?"

"I'm not a patient, and he's expecting me."

"OK, you can wait for the doctor in his office. I'll walk you there and let you in."

I made myself comfortable on the sofa in the doctor's office while I waited for his arrival. It was cool in his office. I was wearing a sleeveless, form-fitting dress, the color of ice, that fell just above the knee. I couldn't wait to see Alex again. I actually longed to see him. In fact, every part of my body seemed to tingle with excitement at the prospect of being close to him again. I could feel my nipples harden, and there was definitely a *throbbing* sensation down *under*. What this man could do to me!

The doctor walked into his office and smiled at me. "Hello there, Briana. Have you been waiting long?"

"Yes, as a matter of fact I have been waiting long. Too long." I raised one of my legs and placed my high-heeled sandal on the sofa. My legs were spread out, and I leaned back against the sofa. He was still in his scrubs, and he just looked so fuckin' hot. I could hardly control myself. I ran my tongue along my lips, but what I really needed was to lick Alex's mouth. I wanted to lick his lips and slide my tongue in his mouth.

The doctor came to kneel in front of me. "What are you doing here, Briana? Did you come here for some sexual healing?" He slid his hand up my dress. He gently began to stroke me with his thumb, over my panties.

"Baby, you're so ready for me. So wet and delicious."

My hand instinctively went up to cup one of my breasts, and Alex immediately moved it away.

"Oh, no you don't. That's my job."

I looked into his deep, dark eyes and saw the same hunger that I was feeling all over my body. I hungered for him, and I grabbed his face closer to mine so I could finally slip my tongue into his sexy mouth and lick his tongue. His lips were gentle and sensual.

Alex then suddenly got up and began to undress. He never took his eyes off of me. He was completely naked. *He was so big.* I wanted him inside of me, but I also needed to take his manhood in my mouth. He understood what I wanted and sat on the couch as I moved down on bended knees before him. He was beautiful, and I reached for him so that I could stroke him. It didn't last long, though, because I really just wanted his cock, *my cock*, in my hungry, greedy mouth. I sucked him hard. My need was urgent, and he tasted so good. *Best damn lollipop that I've ever had, and won't promote tooth decay!* He liked it, and he groaned a deep, sexual sound. He then caressed my cheek with his finger.

"Briana, get undressed." His voice was low, a little groggy, and he was a little out of breath. He sounded so sexy.

I still wanted to suck him, but I got up and slowly began to undress. I was lightheaded, and so excited. I slipped my dress off and stood back so that he could look at me in my bra and panties. I cupped one breast with one hand, and with my other hand I stroked my wet, quivering pussy.

Alex stood up and came toward me. "I told you, that's my job." He pulled me up against him, grabbed my ass with both of his hands, and licked my lips. He took off my bra, and he bent a little so he could kiss my pussy through my panties. He then tugged at my panties with his teeth as he began to slide them off of me.

He led me to the big armchair behind his desk, while kissing me and feeling my body with his hands. He sat on the chair and placed me on top of him. I sat on him with my legs spread out wide. Alex sucked my nipples, gently at first, and then harder. He licked all around my nipples with his wet, sexy tongue. And then I felt his big cock slowly make its way inside of me. I arched my upper body backwards as he continued to lick my nipples. He grabbed my ass with both of his hands as he eased his big, hot cock completely inside of me.

"This is good, Briana." He continued to fuck me, slowly and firmly. "Do you like this? Is this good for you, baby?"

I ran my tongue along his lips. I couldn't control my groaning. "This is *so good* for me. You know how to fuck me so good, Alex."

With clenched teeth, he was barely able to say, "Briana, I'm gonna come. Are you ready?"

"I'm so ready, baby. Come for me, I need you to come for me!"

"Briana, are you sleeping? Briana. Briana!" Dr. Ferrante had walked into the office at the Foundation and was stroking my hair. I had been sitting at his desk, doing some work on the computer, and I must have dozed off. I looked up to find him smiling down at me. If only he knew what I had been dreaming about.

"You must really be tired if you fell asleep like

that." He almost looked a little concerned. "Maybe you're overdoing things a little. Why don't you go on home now and get some rest."

"*Ah*, I'm fine. I'm not even sure that I was asleep. I was doing some research on possible fundraising activities that I'd like to implement. This chair is just so comfy." And I was just so embarrassed.

"Well, at least you seemed to be having a good dream."

"Oh yeah, why do you say that? What did I say?" Did he hear me? *Oh my goodness.*

"Nothing coherent, don't worry." He had a grin on his face. "Although you *were* making some delicious, guttural sounds. What were you dreaming about, Briana?"

I was dreaming about fucking your brains out. I always dream about you, day or night. "I don't know what you're talking about, Dr. Ferrante. I don't even recall falling asleep, let alone dreaming about anything in particular. What are you doing here, anyways? Shouldn't you be at the hospital?"

I had begun doing some work at the Foundation a little over a month ago, and this was only my second time running into him. I pop in and out as much as I can but still have my other responsibilities to tend to. The doctor is at the hospital most days, so I really wasn't expecting to see him. Boy, was he ever a sight for sore eyes. He was wearing a black, slim-fit, polo-style short-sleeved shirt that really seemed to emphasize his broad, fit torso. His dress slacks were light grey, and they too were slim fit, which once again showed off his beautiful body. He really knew how to dress to take full advantage of what was so generously given to him from God.

"I was at a medical conference, and it ran a little longer than expected."

"Alex, are you in there?" A tall, beautiful, red-haired woman walked into the office.

"Yes, Lana. I'm in here." The doctor looked at me, and I tried to hide the look of disappointment on my face.

"Briana, this is Lana, a friend of mine." The redhead came over to the desk and shook my hand. She then moved next to Alex and slipped her arm in the crook of his.

"Are you going to be long, Alex honey? I'm just famished."

The doctor looked down at the redhead, and the smile that he gave her made me feel like a part of my heart had been ripped out.

"We can leave right away, Lana." He then turned to me and from his expression I could tell that I must've looked upset. Well, I was upset. I had just had a very sexy dream about him, and I awoke to find the object of all my desires with another woman.

"Briana, please join us for dinner." The redhead looked just as shocked as I was.

"Thank you, Dr. Ferrante, but I can't." A look of relief crossed the redhead's face.

"Oh, come on now, you need to eat. You can

even pick the restaurant."

The way he asked just made me seem so pathetic. Like I couldn't possibly already have dinner plans, much less with a man.

"Yes, you are right, I do need to eat. But I already have dinner plans. Thank you again, though." Actually, I wasn't lying. My plan was to cook dinner, and eat it with my children, Marco and Elisa.

"Lana, why don't you go ahead and wait for me in the car. I just need to grab a file and I'll be there in a few minutes."

Once the redhead was out of the office, the doctor turned to me and sat on the edge of his desk.

"Are you OK, Briana? You seem a little upset."

"I'm fine."

"Are you really? Briana, does it bother you to see me with other women?"

"Dr. Ferrante! Really?" That feeling of panic was starting to creep in again.

"Briana, you once had romantic feelings about me."

I could see that he felt pity for me.

"It's OK; you don't have to deny it. Do you still feel that way?"

My first reaction was to lie, but somehow, I just couldn't. In fact, I couldn't even speak.

"Briana?"

I took a deep breath and raised my head high. I had nothing to feel ashamed about. We feel what we feel, and I guess we can't really change that, but we need to be honest about our feelings. "Dr. Ferrante, nothing has changed for me."

The doctor got up, a strange look on his face. "I'm not looking for a serious relationship, Briana. You're a very charming, beautiful woman, but..." I interrupted him because I couldn't bear to hear more.

"Please don't, Dr. Ferrante. I have absolutely no expectations from you. I won't lie; I think that you are the complete package." There were a few awkward moments of silence, but then I continued. "I am forever grateful to you for helping my mom out with her lung cancer, and I have the utmost respect for you. But like I said, I don't expect anything from you. Now, I believe your friend is waiting for you in the car, so don't keep her waiting any longer."

"Briana, are *we* OK?"

"Of course we're OK. Now go! *Please...go.*"

Once I was sure that he was gone, and I saw his car drive away from the office, I just couldn't control myself any longer. I let my tears out and I couldn't stop. It hurt so much.

14

Oh My Beautiful Gangsta...

occo's book was coming along. I was really enjoying writing with him. Rocco is creative and has such good ideas. His stories show how hypocritical and fake some people really are. We naturally look down our noses at people that use their *muscles* to persuade or influence certain business dealings. We like to call them dirty thugs, gangsters, mobsters. But what about the legitimate but dirty businessmen, lawyers, politicians, and other wealthier members of society that hide behind their spotless reputations, paid for with their old money, and take part in acts that are just unthinkable and perverse? I have more respect for someone who doesn't hide who he is. You know just what to expect from people like that. It's those that pretend to be pillars of morality, but are far from it, that make me sick to my stomach.

Rocco was lying down on the sofa in his office, reading the last few pages that we had worked on from his book. He was rubbing his scar with his finger, deeply concentrating on his work. I liked watching him when he didn't know it. He was interesting. I wondered about his life, what he did, what deep, dark secrets he had. He warned me on a number of occasions that he was badass and I should really stay away from him. *Like I could?* He pretty much forced me to get involved with him and his book. Of course now that I know him, I don't want to stay away. I want to work with him. He's smart and I'm learning a lot from him. The person that I now know is so very different from the badass Rocco that he claims to be. Who's the real Rocco? Is he the caring, well-spoken, educated, business-savvy gentleman, or is he indeed the gangster, albeit one with a heart? Maybe he's both. *Maybe he is both indeed.*

I got myself a Coke from the fridge in Rocco's office. I was still staring at Rocco when I was walking back to the sofa where we were working. I was so focused on my own thoughts about Rocco that I didn't notice his shoes by the side of the sofa. I tripped over them, of course, and landed right on top of him, my Coke splattering all over his clean white shirt.

"OOOH, my goodness, I'm so sorry."

I heard Rocco's intake of breath, but he didn't move an inch. He was cool and laughed a little. "Honey, if you wanted my attention, you should've just said so. Just teasing you. Don't worry about it. I've got some extra shirts in my closet here in the office."

I managed to get my clumsy body off of him. I just felt so foolish. His shirt was ruined. He was soaked. He laughed as he looked down at himself, proceeded to remove the ruined wet shirt, and walked over to the closet to get another crisp, clean shirt.

The closet was filled with at least fifteen white long-sleeved shirts. "You never know when you'll need an emergency clean shirt while you're at the office!" He said this jokingly as he noticed my shocked expression at seeing his closet. When he stood in front of his closet, shirt still off and back to me, my eyes immediately focused on some scars that he had on his shoulders. Well, not immediately. What I did notice immediately was how fit he really was. Wow, Rocco sure was broad, lean, and toned. He was cut, alright! I guess thinking of him as *cut* really helped me focus on the actual cuts on his body. Without thinking, I began to approach him. As if possessed, my hand went out to touch one of the scars on his shoulder.

"Hey, what are you doing there?" He turned to

face me, a look of surprise in his eyes and a grin on his face, and he grabbed my hand to stop me from touching him. He didn't let go of my hand, though. With his other hand, he lifted my chin so that I could look up at him, into his steel-grey eyes.

"What happened to you, Rocco?" I said in barely a whisper. "Who hurt you?" I was visibly upset and scarcely able to ask him my questions.

"Don't look at me like that, Briana. You look like you want to cry, and you shouldn't waste any tears on me. Look at me! I'll admit that life wasn't always a bed of roses for me, but look at me now. I turned out pretty good! I'm educated, rich, and successful. What more could I ask for?"

I did want to cry, but I wouldn't, because I knew that it would really bother Rocco. Also, I didn't want him to know that I felt sorry for him. What more could he ask for? How about true happiness and love? He was obviously physically hurt in his life. His heart had also been hurt when his beloved Angela passed away. He'd suffered a lot of pain in his life, and I'm sure that I don't even know the half of it.

I was caught up in emotions, and my "strong Rocco" suddenly became my "hurt Rocco." But I don't know what Rocco's excuse was. With his hand still holding up my chin, Rocco lowered his head to mine and kissed me on the lips. It was brief.

After the kiss, I stepped away from him. We just looked at each other. The inevitable feeling of awkwardness never came. Instead of feeling awkward, I suddenly felt like laughing. At first I tried to suppress my laughter, but I found that I couldn't keep it in. I just let it out. I laughed, and I laughed. I laughed so hard I thought I would pee in my pants. And Rocco laughed along with me.

"Yeah, I don't know what that was about, but let's just blame it on fatigue and forget about it. I'm not really into kissing my *sister*!"

"Fine by me, *bro*!"

After that, well, work was pretty much over for the day. I left Rocco's office and headed for home, to my kids. Marco and Elisa always bring me back to reality. I needed to get home, because I was feeling really confused and lost. What had happened back there? I touched Rocco's naked torso, and we kissed. *How the hell did that happen!*

15

Rocco

Rocco was leaning against the window of his office, watching as Briana drove away. He could still feel her gentle touch on his skin. *We kissed! How the hell did that happen!*

Rocco was feeling tired. It had been a long week, and he was glad that it was over. He was pleased with how his investments were performing. He sure did have a keen eye for investing and he just seemed to feel it in his gut when something really good came along.

He left his office, slipped into his car, and headed for home. He looked at the soiled shirt crumpled up into a ball in the passenger seat of his car. Briana was so clumsy. He had seen her on several occasions stumble her way into a room. He had told her so many times to slow down. She was always in a hurry, trying to do too many things at once. He was afraid that one day she would fall and hurt herself.

Briana. Kind, dependable, and loyal Briana. She was also strong, tough, and sharp as a whip. God help anyone who underestimated her many talents. Her touch on his shoulder did take him by surprise. And what was he doing kissing her? Still, she hadn't stopped him. He cared about Briana, and he valued her friendship. He had been around long enough to know that there aren't too many people that can truly be trusted. He needed to protect their friendship, and he wouldn't risk losing it. Besides, Briana wasn't the type to just fuck around with. There was plenty of hot pussy around for that. He preferred blondes with big tits, but he wouldn't turn down a hot pussy if she didn't possess his preferred traits. He did have one strict rule though. A woman with a brain would simply not do for him. He wasn't looking for love, just a sweet warm place to welcome his cock whenever he was in the mood. He never had any trouble finding that.

He'd met Briana under pretty shitty circumstances, but they were now close friends. Rocco felt very protective of her. Briana was strong and smart, but she was naïve and too trusting. She was an easy target for the right sicko, and God knows there are plenty of sickos out there. She worked hard and lived to take care of her two kids. It began to matter to him what she thought of him. Sometimes he would notice her watching him when she thought that he wasn't aware, and he wondered what she was thinking.

He was nearly home when his cell phone rang. It was Salvatore Costa calling. *Uncle Sal.* Rocco thought of him as an uncle, although they weren't even related.

"Uncle Sal, how are you?"

"Good, good, Rocky. Why haven't I seen you in so long? Is something the matter with you? You sick or something?"

"No, I'm good. I saw you last Sunday. That was just the other day!"

"But you haven't called, not even once, and your aunt Marina said she tried calling you but you haven't returned any of her messages. My boy, we worry about you and we want to hear that you're OK."

"Yeah, I got Zia Marina's messages. I've been really busy and I guess I just forgot to return her calls. I'll call her later on." *Seriously, I just saw them, and still if I don't speak to them at least every second day they begin to freak out on me. I guess I shouldn't complain. Family can be a pain, but I'm lucky to have them. I owe them everything.*

"OK, I'm happy to hear your voice, Rocky. I'll see you for lunch on Sunday, and please, don't forget to call your aunt."

"Sure, Uncle Sal, see you then."

Salvatore and Marina Costa took Rocco into their home and welcomed him into their family when he was just twelve years old. Rocco's mom had just died, and Rocco didn't have anybody else to care for him.

Rocco first met the Costa family through his best school buddy, Vincent, who happened to be Sal's oldest son. Rocco and Vincent were inseparable. They had a lot in common. Sports, school, same taste in girls. Rocco's mom was always working, so he spent a lot of time at Vincent's house. He liked it there. His parents were so warm and giving. "Have something to eat, Rocco. Make yourself at home," they would always say. Aunt Marina, Zia, always had something really delicious cooking in the kitchen. She was kind and offered hugs easily. Uncle Sal was always friendly, asking questions about what they were doing in school and giving advice about the importance of doing well and making something of yourself. It was obvious that he was a strong man, but Rocco just couldn't believe some of the rumors going around about Vincent's dad being a mobster. He didn't look like the stereotypical Italian American mobster that we always see on television. He was smart, and although he absolutely had an accent when he spoke, it just added to his charm and made him seem harmless. He was a businessman. A successful one at that. He owned several small businesses in town, and he had just begun to import his own brand of olive oil from Italy. Vincent never said anything about the rumors, and Rocco never asked him about them.

Rocco loved his mom very much, and it killed him that she worked so hard. His dad ran out on them when he was just a baby. They never heard from him, and he was presumed dead. Rocco's mom, Kiara, was a young, pretty mom who worked constantly to try and give her little boy all the best in life. The *best* for her meant making sure that Rocco had enough healthy food to eat every day, a warm, safe bed to sleep in at night, clean clothes to wear, and a good school that would provide him with an education. It wasn't easy for her though, and she often didn't sleep at night worrying about making enough money to pay for all the bills. By day she worked as a legal assistant for a respected *asshole lawyer*, and by night she worked as a waitress in the neighborhood diner. The sleazy prick lawyer, Fred Amar, had a thing for Kiara, and he constantly made sexual advances toward her. She hated him, but with very few options available to her, she had patiently resigned herself to going about her days, trying to work while fighting off the asshole's disgusting advances.

Thinking about his early days and about his mom always made him feel on edge. Once he was finally in his home, a good shower was what Rocco needed. Actually, what he needed was some pussy, but he really didn't feel like going out. He decided that he would call Valerie to come over. Yeah, she was just what he needed tonight. When he was done with his shower, he quickly dressed in some faded blue jeans and a black T-shirt. He placed his call to Valerie, and she would be there within the hour.

Valerie. Yeah, she never disappointed. Always ready and willing to have a wild time. He had seen her on several occasions. He usually didn't like to revisit the same pussy more than a couple of times, but he made the exception for Valerie's juicy body. He was getting hard just thinking about her big tits. And that ass of hers, well, he couldn't wait to slide his cock inside of her, while holding on to her sexy, round, smooth ass. Still, as hot as she was, he never wanted her around after they were done fucking. It actually bothered him to spend time with any of his women after the fucking was over with. The women that he slept with were hot, alright, but so shallow and empty. Funny, he realized that the women that he always chose to fuck with were also the same kind of women that he would've never found appealing in the past. When he was younger, he saw these women as vulgar and tacky. He thought that they were sexy, but certainly not pretty. They looked like they were made to fuck and suck cock. But you didn't actually *kiss* these girls, at least not on the face. Well, Rocco wasn't looking for a pretty face to look at anymore. A juicy body, a hot pussy, and big tits were all he needed now.

The sound of the phone ringing softened his hard-on a little. "Hello."

"Hey, Roc, what's up?"

"Hey, Vinnie. Nothing much, man." *Apart from my dick.* "What's up with you? How's work?" Vincent was a veterinarian, and they were still the best of friends. "And how are Maria and the kids?" Vincent and Rocco spoke almost daily. Vincent was married to a pretty little thing named Maria, and they had three kids together. Maria and Angela had been best friends. Vincent and Maria got married about two months after Angela and Rocco, and they had great plans to get pregnant at the same time and grow old together. All their dreams about private schools for their kids, family vacations taken together, living as neighbors in homes with white picket fences, and, most important of all, Rocco's only chance for real happiness, well, they died along with Angela.

Rocco and Vincent spoke frequently, so their calls were very brief. Simple, short, and to the point.

"Rocco, will I see you on Sunday?"

"Sure, Vinnie. I'll see you then. Kiss Maria and the kids for me, OK."

What a great friend Vincent had turned out to be. When Vinnie was a kid, he was a little scrawny and a little sickly. He suffered from so many allergies, and his asthma kept him from playing certain sports. Some of the boys tried to target Vinnie and bully him. Kids could be so mean. Even as a child, Rocco couldn't stand bullies. What cowards! Vincent was the smartest kid in class, and he was also the nicest. So Rocco had made it his personal mission to become Vinnie's friend and *bodyguard*. At twelve years old, Rocco was tall for his age and was as strong as an ox. Nobody dared to even think of Vinnie as a punching bag after Rocco started hanging out with him. The two boys were inseparable, and they always looked out for one another. They've been the best of friends ever since.

Valerie arrived a little earlier than expected. *Eager little pussy!* She was wearing a tight mini dress that left nothing to the imagination. She looked like a tramp, and it was just what he wanted. Her tits were practically spilling out of her dress. They looked so good to Rocco. She looked so good to him. She looked tacky and very fuckable. Without wasting any more time, Rocco led Valerie to a bedroom, where he would really enjoy fucking her tits and her juicy round ass.

Rocco woke up the next morning feeling refreshed. He'd had a really good night's sleep. Valerie was just what the doctor had ordered. She had a very fuckable pussy indeed. But like always, once they were done, he was ready for her to leave. As a matter of fact, after the third time that they went at it, he just couldn't stand the sight of her anymore. She pretty much turned him off, and even her big tits disgusted him a little. He was relieved when she finally got dressed and told him that she had a party that she needed to get to.

Rocco decided to have breakfast on his patio. He had a big, beautiful home with a beautifully groomed backyard. So relaxing and peaceful. His housekeeper was off on the weekends, but he was more than capable of preparing his coffee, eggs, bacon, and toast. As he sat and enjoyed his surroundings, he thought about his family. He would see them tomorrow. Oh, they weren't biologically related, but they couldn't be closer or love each other more if they had the same blood running through their veins. He didn't have any biological relatives that he knew of. He never met anyone from his father's family, and his mom was an only child who didn't have any relatives. If not for the Costa family, he would've been alone in this world.

Rocco could still remember how difficult life had become for him and his mom. It was so difficult for Kiara to keep her sleazy boss off of her. Her death never stopped haunting him. Years in therapy made it possible for him to now be able to think about the events of that day. For years he wasn't able to.

It was late, and his mom wasn't home from work yet. She had decided that she was going to quit working for that bastard lawyer Fred Amar. Rocco had confided in Vincent about Kiara's situation at work. When Vincent told his dad, well, he didn't think twice about offering her a job at one of his businesses. Feeling a little uneasy about it all, and given how late it was, Rocco decided to go to his mom's place of work to make sure that things were OK. Although it was a small office, there were other employees that worked for this asshole. Nobody was around. When he noticed that his mom's things were still at her desk, he knew that it was bad.

Rocco opened the door to the backroom and saw his mother lying on the floor, curled up in the fetal position. Fred Amar, respected lawyer and upstanding citizen, had raped Rocco's mother. The prick had beaten and sodomized her and then left her unconscious in a pool of her own blood. Rocco, just twelve years old, afraid and uncertain as to what to do, did the only thing that he could think of. He called Vincent. Within minutes an ambulance was at the office, and both Kiara and Rocco were taken to the hospital. Kiara died two days later as a result of her injuries.

Fred Amar made a public appearance stating that he would not rest until Kiara's rapist and killer was caught and brought to justice. He was never considered a suspect in the murder.

On the one-month anniversary of Kiara's death, Fred Amar was involved in a very bad car crash. He died on impact.

Rocco moved in with Salvatore and Marina Costa after his mother's death. The Costas made sure that Rocco had the best mental health care to help him get through his traumatic experience. They gave him a home and all the luxuries that came along with being a member of the Costa family. Most important of all, they loved Rocco. Although it was never confirmed, Rocco knew that he had Sal to thank for Fred Amar's sudden unexpected death. Rocco had overheard Sal talking to one of his *associates* in his study one day: "That slimy bastard got what he deserved. Nobody hurts a member of my family and gets away with it." Rocco never felt the need to ask. He was simply grateful to Sal for it.

It was such a beautiful day. Warm and dry. Rocco was undecided if he should take a dip in his pool. Of course there was that Pompeii exhibit at the Museum of Science that he had been interested in seeing. Angela would've loved to see it. She was so eager to do *anything,* really. *Angela, so full of life, always positive and filled with so much enthusiasm.* He missed her so much. He had a constant ache in his heart for her. The only thing that got him through life was his belief that he would one day be with her again. He longed to hold her. He smiled as he remembered how her small frame seemed to fit perfectly into his body. She was made for him. They were made for each other. Without Angela, Rocco just went about his life, alive without really living.

Rocco took a walk around his grounds. There were tall lilac bushes all around his backyard. He had them planted because lilacs were one of Angela's favorite flowers. She loved flowers.

With the scorching heat as the deciding factor, Rocco removed his shorts and dove into the pool, completely naked. *To hell with swimming trunks!* Lord knows he had paid plenty for his home so he could have the privacy that he guarded and appreciated. As he came up for air, he thought he could still hear Angela's sweet, bubbly voice, just like on that first day when he met her.

"Hey, you must be Rocco, newest member of the Costa family. I'm Angela, Vinnie's cousin."

When Rocco first moved in with the Costa family, he spent a lot of time at home. They had a beautiful pool, and he really relished in this luxury, having come from a very modest and plain home.

Rocco was still in the pool when Angela sat her thirteen-year-old butt down by the pool and submerged her feet in the water. "I heard so much about you, so I'm glad that we're finally meeting. My family and I moved here just last week, from Vancouver. Bet you can't hold your breath underwater for more than thirty seconds!"

"I'm pretty sure I can," was Rocco's response. "But what do I get if I win the bet?"

Angela burst with bubbly laughter. "I guess you'll just have to trust me enough to wait and see."

He must've fallen in love with her from that very first day, because after that, no girl was ever as pretty, as fun, or as smart as Angela was in Rocco's eyes.

16

I Need You Tonight

Maybe it was the novelty of it, or maybe it was because I felt that I was doing something worthwhile, but I was really enjoying my work at the Foundation. For once in my life, I felt like I was giving back. I was finally *earning* the life that God gave me. What an unexpected turn my life had taken. When Peter entered my life, a black force came along with him that made me miserable. However, I also have my children because of Peter, and if he is the worst thing to ever happen to me, then I have to say that Marco and Elisa really are the greatest pleasure in my life. Because of Peter, I also met Rocco. Although I originally thought of Rocco as the slime of the earth, I now think of him as a trusted and loyal friend. I don't have too many of those, so I appreciate Rocco all the more. However, it shames me to say that with all the blessings in my life, I'm still nursing a broken heart over my sexy Dr. Ferrante.

I see Dr. Ferrante pretty often these days. The hospital where he works is near the Foundation, and he pops in every now and then. I've been there a lot lately, mostly in the early evenings, because of the projects that I've been working on. If I need to be completely honest though, I think that I've also been spending so much time there because I want to see Dr. Ferrante. I must be a sucker for punishment, because he often walks in with a beautiful woman on his arm. He's always with a different woman, she's always gorgeous, and every time my heart breaks a little. I sit quietly at my desk and pretend to be so engrossed in my work while I listen to their flirtatious whispers. He often asks me if I need anything or if I'd like to join him and his friend for dinner. I know he's trying to be polite, but I really wish that he would knock it off with the invites, especially in front of his date, because it just embarrasses me and it makes me look so pathetic. One late afternoon he walked in when I also happened to be there, although it was earlier than usual for me. I had finished working on my column early and had to drop off my kids at their friend's birthday party a couple of streets down from the Foundation.

I was surprised to see that he was alone. He

also wasn't his usual self.

"Well, hello there, Briana. Just the girl I was hoping to see."

I was sitting at my desk, and he made his way toward me. He sat on the edge of my desk.

"Hello, Dr. Ferrante. What are you doing here?"

"Did you forget that I do a lot of work for this foundation, Briana? *My* foundation?"

"No, of course not. I just figured that you'd be in surgery, as you usually are on Friday afternoons."

"Yes, well, I was in surgery but it ended early. Why are *you* here, Briana? Why are you always here?" For a moment the look of sarcasm on his face was replaced by a look of concern, but maybe I just imagined it. "Briana, I think you work too much. You need to have more fun in life before it's too late. What do you say, Briana, wanna have a little fun with me tonight?"

"Dr. Ferrante, what is the matter with you? You're acting a little strange."

He just sat there, with a lazy sexy grin on his face. "Come on, let's have some fun." He then leaned forward and touched my cheek with his finger.

I got up and moved away from him. My cheek burned where his finger touched it. His eyes were so dark and penetrating. His grin was gone, and he just looked at me, and I could tell that he was thinking something over in his mind.

"What's wrong, Doctor, no female companion available for you tonight?"

He laughed, got up from the desk, and came closer to me. "No, not tonight. But like I already said, I was hoping to see *you* tonight. I had a rough day, Briana, and I think that I'd like to spend some time with you."

"But why *me*?" I said the words before I could stop myself. I really didn't want him to see my insecurities, *and he should be so lucky as to spend some time with me!*

"Because I like you, and because you make me laugh. I need some laughter in my life after the day that I've just had."

"So watch a comedy. There's a really good one playing at the cinema not too far from here."

"Briana, my patient died on me today." He became really serious and reached for my hand. "She was so young."

The look in his eyes was heartbreaking. He seemed to really care about the welfare of his patients. It's really rare to see this in a doctor nowadays. Before I knew what I was doing, I leaned forward and with my free hand touched his face. We looked at each other for what seemed like an eternity. He then lowered his head and kissed me, although it wasn't technically a kiss. He just brushed his lips lightly against mine.

"I wanna get drunk tonight. Come with me."

"I can't." I didn't need alcohol. His breath on my mouth was enough to make me feel a little tipsy.

"Yes, you can. I need you tonight. We'll have dinner, and then we'll go to my place for drinks, as I don't intend to get a DUI charge on my *spotless* record."

"No, I really can't. As much as the idea of getting drunk with you appeals to me"—*not!*—"I need to pick up my children from the movies in a couple of hours."

He backed away from me and folded his arms across his chest. He tilted his head to the side. "You must be a great mom."

"I am." I meant for my response to sound playful, but somehow it just sounded very serious.

"I wouldn't expect anything less from you. I remember how attentive you were with your mom when she was in the hospital. I've told you before, Briana, you're a very special person. But now I need you too. Will you care for *me* tonight?"

"Dr. Ferrante…"

He interrupted me. "Alex."

Why did I feel embarrassed to call him by his name? "Alex, you're obviously not yourself today. Maybe you should just go home and get to bed early tonight."

He was grinning now. "Maybe an early night *is* the best thing for me. Will you come tuck me in? Come on, I really need you tonight."

He kept looking at me with a kind of desperation in his eyes. He said that he needed me. What did he need me for? What could I do for him? I wanted to take away his pain and I longed to comfort him. I couldn't answer; I didn't know how to answer him.

"OK, so I'll just stay here, and I'll do some work. I'll order in some food, maybe Chinese. May I have the pleasure of your company for dinner, milady?" he asked, bending forward slightly and asking me the question in a mocking, exaggerated way as if to demonstrate how gentlemanly he could be.

"Yes." My response was immediate. He really had no idea how desperately I wanted to be with him. But I also didn't want to be just another woman for him. And I didn't want to start resenting him for not caring about me in the way that I needed him to.

The food came quickly enough. Alex had two bottles of red wine stashed away in his office, and it didn't take him long to go through them. I only had one glass myself, and it was more than I could handle, especially seeing that I couldn't let my guard down, not with Alex being in the strange mood that he was in.

We ate all the food, and by the end of the second bottle of wine, Alex had moved on to lying down on the sofa in his office. He wasn't as drunk as I would've expected him to be after drinking so much wine. But he was definitely a *little* drunk.

"Come sit with me." It sounded more like an order than a request, but I nonetheless went to sit on the sofa next to him. He seemed a little more relaxed than he had been earlier. His eyes now had a look of sadness about them, rather than the bewildered desperation that I saw in them when he first came in. His grin was no longer mocking, and his speech had become a little slurred. He took hold of my hand and he kept it on his knee as he lay back and rested his head on the arm of the sofa.

"Do you have a lover, Briana?"

"Dr. Ferrante! That's really none of your business." I tried to get up, but he wouldn't let me. He pulled me down, closer to him, with my upper body lying on him.

"Let me go, now."

"No."

"How dare you? Who do you think you are?"

"Why, I'm Dr. Alex Ferrante, esteemed cardiothoracic surgeon, and some even refer to me as 'the great one.'"

He kept me on him with one hand, and he slid his other hand down my back and rested it on my bum. He stroked me there, and as I gasped in horror, he squeezed a little. I'd dreamt about being in an intimate embrace with the "great doctor" so many times, but now that it was actually happening, well, I was just freaking out.

"You're drunk and you don't know what you're doing. HEY, it's me, Briana. I'm not one of your women that will--"

He stopped my words by lightly slapping my behind with his hand.

I was outraged. "How dare you?"

"Quiet!" His voice was firm and commanding.

"Come kiss me."

"You've got to be kidding me? If you think that I'm--"

Once again, he had total disregard for my protests and outrage. He pulled me up higher, closer to him, so that we were face to face.

"I've seen the way that you look at me, Briana. I know that you want me." Yes, I did want him. *And I was humiliated.* But I also loved him. I wanted his body, shamelessly. I wanted to have wild, passionate sex with him, scrubs on or off, on a sofa, bed, desk, you name it, wherever. But I also wanted the tender love-making. And he knew how I felt, and I was indeed humiliated.

"No, sweetheart, don't be embarrassed," he said in response to my obvious discomfort.

"You are so full of yourself. Let me go. I DO NOT WANT THIS." *Oh, but I did.*

With his hand firmly placed on the back of my head, he began to kiss me on my mouth. His lips were surprisingly gentle in comparison to the force that he was using to keep me on him. I felt his tongue slide along my lips, and that's pretty much all it took to make me putty in his hands. I opened my mouth in response. *Oh, I wanted more, so much more.* I too began to kiss him, but I wasn't content with just kissing his lips, however sexy and delicious they were. I slid my tongue in his mouth and had an urgent need to taste him. I ran my tongue along his lips. I licked his tongue, his teeth, and the inside of his mouth. I could taste the wine that he had drunk. And while I was exploring his beautiful mouth, his hands were exploring my body. With one hand still on my bottom, his other hand was now cupping my breast. He reached in through my blouse, underneath my bra, and gently picked at my nipple, causing it to instantly harden underneath his touch. He shifted his body a little, allowing me to now lie completely on him. I could feel his hardness against me. My hand seemed to have a mind of its own as it reached down and began to stroke his manhood through his pants. In response to my touch, he let out a sexy, guttural sound. There was no denying the pleasure that he was obviously feeling.

"You're so sweet." His voice was husky. "You taste so good. This feels so right. You're so beautiful. You feel so good."

I was reveling in his lovemaking and really enjoying his words. I was sure that I was partly unconscious, so when his phone rang, well, I immediately thought that I was just having another one of my dreams about him. But this was no dream. This was really happening, and we were so rudely and cruelly interrupted.

"I'm sorry, sweetie. I have to get it. It might be the hospital calling."

Reality hit me like a ton of bricks. "Of course you need to get it." He kissed me once more, firmly on my mouth, before reaching for his phone. I tried to get up, but he allowed me to move just enough to be able to sit up next to him. He didn't allow me to get up from the sofa. With one arm around me, he kissed my forehead and told me to stay put.

And I needed to get to my kids. *What the hell was I doing?* Alex was feeling bad about losing a patient. He had too much to drink and found himself without a woman for once. He turned to me because I just happened to be there. But I knew that one night with him would never be enough for me. In fact, just one night would probably kill me. He already told me that he wasn't looking for a serious relationship. So this would've been just another night with a different woman for him. And it's not like I really wanted a serious relationship either. I mean, really, it's not like I had such a positive experience with being married that I was dying to dive right back in there. But still, Alex wasn't just any guy. He was the object of all of my fantasies and dreams. He wasn't Mr. Right, he was Mr. Perfect.

I don't know how I didn't notice it right away, but while Alex was on the phone, obviously talking to someone from the hospital, he slid his hand up my skirt. My legs were slightly parted, and his hand began to stroke me over my panties. His eyes on mine, his look intense and smoldering, he slipped his middle finger underneath my panties and gently began to caress me, teasingly. *What the fuck!* He was still on the phone, and I thought that I would faint from the pleasure.

I somehow managed to get his hand out from underneath my skirt just as he finished his call.

He didn't say anything but simply raised my chin with his hand; he lowered his head and kissed me passionately and deeply. It would've been too easy to just let it happen and simply enjoy in the moment. But reality is cruel and it's inevitable. My dilemma was obvious. Have sex with him and lose the object of all of my fantasies. He would not want more than one night with me, and this would kill me, and I would ultimately resent him for it. Or forgo the pleasure of loving him, even for just one night, but then I would be able to hold on to my fantasies that had gotten me through some pretty trying times. I chose to hold on to my fantasies. I wasn't prepared to lose the only man that could get me so wet with just one look.

"I'm sorry. I need to go." I pushed him away with both of my hands. He looked confused, and I managed to get up before he could react.

"What is it, sweetie? Why won't you let me love you?"

Love me? I think *fuck* is a more appropriate word for what he had in mind. Don't get me wrong, every now and then a girl does need a wild, passionate, earth-shattering fucking. But this was *my* Dr. Ferrante, and a one-time-only fucking simply would not do.

"You had a rough day and you had a little too much to drink. And I need to get to my kids. So let's just put a stop to this now, before it's too late and we're left with nothing but regrets."

Alex sat there, looking at me, and I saw the

look on his face turn from confusion to under-standing. He ran his fingers through his hair trying to put it back into place. I felt a little embarrassed as I realized that I was the one that had made a mess out of it.

"You're probably right." He was looking a little tired, and a lot sober.

"Doctor…Alex…can I drive you home?" Although he certainly seemed sober, he still wasn't in a position to drive himself anywhere.

"That's not necessary, thank you. I'll grab a cab. I live close by."

"OK, well, I really should be going now. My kids are waiting for me."

"Go ahead, Briana. Have a good night."

"Good night." *I'll be dreaming about you,* I thought to myself as I walked out.

I knew that sleep was not going to come easy for me that night. I lay in bed and just kept going over what had happened with Dr. Ferrante. He was a strong lover, and gentle. As giving and self-less in bed as he was in his work. He was just as I had imagined him to be in my dreams. I could still smell his masculine scent on my skin. I felt like a child because I wouldn't shower before getting into bed. I didn't want to wash away his scent or the feel of his hands on my body.

And then my cell phone rang, alerting me to an incoming text message. I just knew that it was him.

"Are you awake?"

That was all that he asked.
I responded in similar fashion.

"Yes, I'm awake. Glad to see that you made it home OK."

"Worried about me, were you?"

"Slightly."

"Maybe if we hadn't left things unfinished, we'd both be sleeping by now. And I don't really like to take cold showers."

"I'm sure you'll survive."

"I'm not so sure. Thank you for having dinner with me. Sweet dreams."

"Sweet dreams."

Mine will be of you, of course.
And with that, I closed my eyes and drifted off to sleep.

17

You Must've Been Photoshopped!

Needless to say, I woke up the next morning feeling exhausted and a little anxious. I was confused, a little happy, and sad all at the same time. Maybe the best way to approach what had happened the night before was to avoid overanalyzing it.

I would see Dr. Ferrante again today. I wasn't sure how I would feel once I saw him, or how he'd react to seeing me. Rocco was having a party at his home, and he'd asked me to attend. I refused at first, telling him that I didn't think that it was a good idea. But when he kept asking me and pressuring me, well, eventually I figured why not. I needed to start working on getting a social life. I took care of my kids, and I worked. Not much time for anything else, but it was starting to get me down. Rocco said that there would be about fifty people attending, and the party would mainly be held outdoors. He also mentioned that Dr. Ferrante would be attending as well.

It had been a hot and humid Saturday, and I'd spent most of the day swimming with my kids in my mom's pool. I wanted to get my hair done at the salon, but with the heavy humidity it would've been useless to get it straightened. So by late afternoon, I headed for home to begin getting ready for Rocco's party. I decided to wear a strapless little gold-and-cream dress. My shoes were strappy, gold high heels. My hair lay loose about my shoulders, and it curled naturally. Spending the day in the sun had allowed for my skin to have a lightly tanned, sun-kissed glow to it. I was happy with my appearance, and it helped boost my self-confidence.

Huge and elegantly furnished, Rocco's home was beautiful. It suited Rocco. He was always dressed so well, and his home was furnished in accordance with his impeccable taste. I couldn't help but feel a little sad for Rocco, though. He should be living in this beautiful home with a woman that he loves. A woman who loves *him* deeply. Lord knows he's good-looking enough to have any woman by his side. He's strong, smart and, yes, he's sexy.

Ever since that day in his office when we kissed, images of his perfectly fit body keep popping into my mind. It's a little disconcerting for me. Rocco is my friend, and I feel genuine affection for him. I don't want to start seeing him as a sexual being.

Rocco introduced me to several guests. I met Vincent and Maria, who both seemed so very nice. When I was standing in front of a beautiful portrait of Rocco's late wife, Maria confided in me that she also greatly missed Angela, but it troubled her that Rocco never remarried or got into a serious relationship with anyone else.

"You know, Briana, what Angela and Rocco had was special, but it's just not normal that he's buried his heart with her. Vinnie and I just want to see him happy again. He deserves it, and he's had so little happiness in his life."

"I would love to see him find some happiness too. I'm sure Rocco will love again, when he meets the right person." It was nice to see that Rocco had a good family and that they loved him.

"Angela was one in a million. She was my best friend, you know, and I miss her too. I still remember when we were kids, just thirteen years old or so. We were all at Vinnie's house, by the pool, and Angela pulled me to the side. She was all giddy and happy, and she declared to me on that very same day that she would one day marry Rocco. She said that he was the one, her soul mate. I do believe that she was right. But she's dead, and Rocco needs to move on."

I was relieved when Rocco came to get me so that he could introduce me to some other guests. The conversation with Maria was beginning to make me feel a little too sad.

"Your conversation with Maria seemed a little intense. Is everything OK?" Rocco had asked me, in a low voice close to my ear. "What were you talking about?"

"You." Rocco looked surprised and maybe even a little upset.

"I see. It's not nice to gossip about a supposed friend, Briana." He now just looked annoyed.

I grabbed onto his arm as he was about to turn away from me. Was he upset with me? And just then Dr. Ferrante was making his way toward us.

"Hello, Briana." He barely looked at me. "Rocco, there you are. Great party, and *interesting* guests." He pretended to clear his throat, grinned, and nodded in the direction of four beautiful women that were obviously into Alex and openly admiring him.

"Hey, Alex. Really glad you could come. Let me introduce you to some of my clients."

I reached out once again to Rocco and held onto his hand. "Wait, Rocco. We were in the middle of a discussion. I'm sure Dr. Ferrante could find his own way and help himself." I didn't mean it to, but it came out so bitchy. Alex must have thought that it sounded bitchy as well, because he no longer grinned but just looked at me with a raised eyebrow.

"Don't be such a silly child, Briana. Would you have me be rude to my guests? Now go mingle a little. Who knows, you might even meet a man tonight." Rocco then grabbed Alex and led him toward his "groupies."

I was left by myself, fuming and humiliated. How could he speak to me in that way, and in front of Dr. Ferrante? I just stood there like a fool. Rocco then looked at me from his end of the room, and our eyes locked. I thought that I would cry. Instead, I just turned around and made my way for the door. I was going to leave. I was so tired of being treated like shit by everybody in my life. Everyone ultimately shits on me. Even Rocco. Fuck him! Fuck Alex! Fuck everyone!

I had made my way outdoors, and I was so glad that I hadn't used the valet service. I was walking, trying to remember just where the hell I had parked my car.

"Briana! Briana, wait!" Rocco was running toward me. He caught up to me in no time. This time *he* grabbed my arm and spun me around.

"Just where the hell do you think you're going? *Briana?*" His voice softened. "You're crying."

"I'm not crying. And fuck you! Let go of me, you brute! Who do you think you are? Why do you think that it's OK to speak to me like that? WHY?" My body was shaking at this point, and I was sobbing. Rocco wore an expression of grief. He then moaned deeply, and he took me in his arms. He buried his face in my hair.

"I'm so sorry, honey. Stop crying. Please, I can't stand it. I don't know what's wrong with me. I am a brute, you're right."

"Why, Rocco? It's like you want to hurt me sometimes. *Why?*" He was stroking my hair with one hand and rubbing my arm with his other.

"I have a lot of baggage, Briana. It's no excuse, I know. When you told me that you were talking to Maria about me, well, I think that I felt betrayed by you. You're supposed to be *my* friend, and you should have *my* back. You shouldn't be gossiping about me. And honestly, I think that I was afraid of what you might learn about me. You mean a lot to me, Briana. I don't want to lose you. One day you'll learn just how awful I really am, and then you'll leave me. And then who's going to help me with my book?"

His pathetic attempt at humor actually got a chuckle out of me.

He took a tissue out of his pocket and wiped my tears. He stayed with me until my nose was no longer red, my eyes were no longer puffy, and it was no longer obvious that I had been crying. We then went back inside to the party.

Rocco was a good host, and he mingled with the endless stream of guests in his home. I saw him on several occasions watching me from one end of the room or the other. He would just smile, or wink at me. I think he felt badly about what had happened, and he was feeling guilty.

I realized that *some guy* that I had just met

was still talking to me about *something*. I hadn't been paying any attention to him, and his voice was beginning to get on my nerves. "Please excuse me. I need to get some fresh air." I said and made my way outdoors once again, this time in Rocco's backyard. His land seemed to be never-ending. I walked past his pool and beyond where many guests were lingering, and I went to sit on a bench overlooking a small pond. I was enjoying the serenity of this little piece of paradise that was Rocco's own backyard.

"It's nice here, isn't it?"

I hadn't even heard Dr. Ferrante as he came to sit next to me. "Oh, it's you. Yes, it's very nice here." I wanted to go on to say that I thought that Rocco's house was beautiful, but God forbid Rocco should learn of it and think that I was *gossiping* about him! Of course, maybe I should have been grateful to Rocco for the little incident back there, as it kept me from obsessing about Alex for a little while. But now here he was, sitting next to me.

"I didn't hear you coming. Or maybe I just didn't recognize you without your *entourage*!"

"Don't be naughty!" He tapped the tip of my nose with his finger, looking a little amused. I instinctively slapped his finger away. "Or maybe your bad behavior today is due to your sexual frustration at leaving things unfinished yesterday. We can fix that, you know."

"Oh, why don't you just go pour your charm over some woman that actually cares?" I spat the words out at him, surprising myself as well as Alex. Maybe I *was* sexually frustrated. Who was I kidding? I couldn't remember the last time that I'd had sex, and I'd gotten really close to it yesterday with none other than the man of my dreams. Oh yeah, I was frustrated, alright!

Dr. Ferrante then grabbed hold of my shoulders and drew me close to him. "I'm beginning to think that maybe I've been wrong about you all of this time, treating you with kid gloves, afraid of hurting a delicate, fragile creature."

"Don't touch me!" I tried to push at his chest with my hands, but Alex just held me tighter.

Grinning now, he spoke really close to my lips, almost touching them but not quite. "A fragile creature? I think not! *You are a little wildcat.* I like that!"

"Shut up! Why don't you just go away and find someone who needs a vital organ ripped out of them!"

He was openly laughing now. "No, I think I'll stay right here. I like the *vital organs* that are right next to me."

"Let go of me."

"No."

"Now!"

"Kiss me first."

"Never!"

This really amused Alex. His eyes were mocking, and this really annoyed me, but then I made the mistake of looking at his mouth. It's just so fuckin' sexy. His lips are shapely and strong and so tender. He brushed his lips against mine. I didn't respond, although I was dying to lick him dry.

He suddenly looked serious. "I didn't sleep at all last night, Briana. I couldn't stop thinking about you. Did you know that you make delicious little sounds when you're making love?"

"Making love? Is that what you call what we were doing?"

"What should I call it, then?" He backed away from me a little, although he still held me in his arms. "I don't understand this behavior from you, Briana. Are you still the same sweet, charming woman who sent me countless witty texts while I was treating your mom? Where's the woman that looked excited to see me and eagerly hung on to my every word when I did my rounds?"

"You are just so full of yourself! Who says that I was excited to see you? And if I *was* excited, it was because I was anxious to hear what you had to say about my mom's condition, that's all. It wasn't about you."

"Really? I'm sure that sounds lame, even to you."

If looks could kill, then he'd be dead. I was embarrassed and furious that he would use that against me. But he was right. I had the hots for him, and we both knew it.

"You know, it's OK to admit to feeling attracted to someone, sweetheart." If he had sounded sarcastic or mocking, then I would've really been upset. But he just sounded sincere.

"You really flatter yourself, you know. Must be because you always have so many willing stupid women around to boost that doctor's ego of yours."

"So that's it, then? That sweet girl with the flirtatious smile and witty sense of humor is gone, and in her place is this wildcat with a sharp little tongue. I like it!" And then he laughed again. He also pulled me closer and kissed me.

I knew that I should've been stronger. I should've pushed him away, but I just couldn't. He kept kissing me. He slid his tongue in my mouth, and I welcomed it. I didn't just let him kiss me; I kissed him too. The kiss went on and on. Alex finally raised his head, but only to lower it again as he lay kisses all over my face and forehead.

"It feels great doesn't it? We're so *electric* together! Do you feel it too?"

I was barely able to respond. "Yeah, *electric*." *Now shut up and kiss me, you blubbering fool*!

"Sweetie, anyone looking our way would think that we're just a couple of lucky people, hopelessly in love, and unashamedly in lust with one another." He chuckled a little.

He found this amusing, while it just saddened me. I really was in love with him, and unashamedly in lust with him.

"You find this funny, don't you?"

I tried hard to sound nonchalant instead of serious. "You could play out this scene every night if you wanted to. You have enough willing women around to work with you."

"There are always plenty of women around, but this scene could only work with you." He kissed me once again. "Come home with me tonight."

"I can't."

"Is it because of your kids? Do you need to pick them up somewhere?"

My kids were safe and sound, spending the night at my mom's. "No, it's not that. Alex, if I come home with you tonight, what happens next? What about tomorrow?"

His back stiffened, and he suddenly looked really serious. "I already care about you, Briana, but I don't think that I can offer you what you're looking for."

"And just what do you think that I'm looking for, Alex?"

"I was married once, Briana, and I wasn't very good at it. I don't wish to repeat that mistake. Look, like I said, I care about you and I like you a lot. I respect you, so I would never do anything to intentionally hurt you. That's why I will always be honest with you. I enjoy being with you and talking with you. But I also think that you're beautiful, and *so hot*. I really want to be with you, sexually. I think that we'd be great together. I know that you feel the sparks between us. So what's wrong with simply enjoying each other's company every now and then?"

"So what you're proposing is getting together,

whenever the mood strikes us, and having sex, and--"

"Not *just* having sex, Briana. We could go for dinner, go to an art exhibit, enjoy each other's company, and well, yes, also have sex. I want you, and I know that you want me too. Don't get me wrong, at first I didn't think that this type of relationship could be possible between us, but after last night... well, quite frankly, you were responsible for giving me the biggest hard-on. I woke up this morning in a terrible mood, and all I could think about was you."

"So you had a hard-on, and now you want to have a casual sexual relationship with me?" *Wow! He's clueless and insulting.* I didn't really know what I felt, or how I should feel. I was hurt, but strangely enough, hearing him call me *hot* eased my pain a little, believe it or not. That was pathetic even for me.

"I was married too once, and I don't wish to repeat that disaster again either. I'm not really sure what I'm looking for, quite honestly, but I do know that having a casual sexual relationship with you is not the answer." I could never have sex with this man one night, only to see him with another woman on another. Maybe if I didn't love him I could give in. But I had loved him and dreamed about him for too long to give it all up for casual sex. After all, in my fantasies about him, I'm everything that he needs. How could I accept anything less from him in reality?

"Seeing that you're being so honest with me, I will be the same with you. I do want you, and you know it. I've wanted you for so long. But when I look at you, I *see* and I guess I *want* the complete picture. You make me want to grab you, tear off your clothes, and have my way with you. I know, shameless." I added that in at his exaggerated look of shock. "But I also want to live a normal life with you. I want to have nice dinners at home with you, and I want to spend relaxing Sunday afternoons lying next to you on the sofa reading a really good book and sharing it with you. And I especially do not want to share you with any other woman. You need to be mine, completely, or I can't be with you. I can't be your part-time lover."

We sat there for a while in silence. He then took my hand, kissed it, and just held it against his mouth.

"Well now, there you are. Briana, I've been looking all over for you." Rocco was coming toward us. He didn't look too pleased to see us sitting in the dark. "At first I thought that you left the party, but then I saw that your car is still parked out front. What are you guys doing here?"

"We're just talking and enjoying how peaceful it is out here," Alex casually responded.

"Alex, I think some of your *friends* are probably wondering where you are and why you've decided to abandon them." Rocco wasn't his usual playful self with Alex. He sounded a little too serious.

"Actually, Rocco, they're your friends. I just met them, and I'm not really interested in that tonight. I've been lucky enough to have the pleasure of Briana's company, but maybe we *should* go back inside now." Alex turned to me and took my hand as he went to get up. "After all, I think that we should have something to eat, have a drink, and, Briana, you haven't danced with me yet tonight."

I was speechless, and the look on Rocco's face kept me that way.

Alex walked past Rocco, all the while holding my hand and keeping me next to him. Rocco followed behind, looking annoyed as hell. I don't know what his problem was, but he just looked so dark and bothered.

Alex didn't leave my side for most of the night. After the intense conversation that we'd had earlier, he was now acting surprisingly sweet and attentive. I noticed women look at him, flirting, but Alex didn't pay any attention to them. He had eyes only for me. I guess he had decided that I was his "flavor of choice" for the night. *That must have been some hard-on that he had last night!* I just let myself enjoy the attention, because I knew that it wouldn't last long.

I was surprised to see Rocco leaning against the wall outside the powder room when I came out of it later that evening. "Oh, Rocco, have you been waiting long? Had I known that you were waiting to use the restroom I wouldn't have taken so long."

Rocco rolled his eyes and shook his head. "Ah, Briana, there are seven bathrooms in this house. If I needed to use the bathroom, I wouldn't be waiting outside this door like some idiot!"

"What is it with you tonight, Rocco? Tell me what's wrong." I reached for him and touched his hand.

Rocco looked down at my hand on his. He then looked at me and sighed. "I don't want to see you get hurt. You're an easy target, Briana! You have two kids and yet you're as naïve and innocent as a little girl. I don't want anyone taking advantage of your good nature and your kind heart."

"Who's going to hurt me, Rocco? I mean really, I've already been forced into a relationship with a *gangsta,* so what else could happen to me?"

Laughing, Rocco grabbed my hand and brought it to his mouth. He kissed my hand and then looked at me with a sad expression on his face.

"I was wrong to involve you in my life, with a gangster, or a *gangsta*, as you put it."

"Ah, but you are a *gangsta* with a heart. And Rocco, I know that you have the kindest heart underneath that rough and tough exterior. You can't fool me, my friend."

"Just don't be so trusting of everyone, Briana. You need to be a little harder, tougher."

"Is this about Dr. Ferrante? Because if it is, you have nothing to worry about. Dr. Ferrante will always mean a lot to me, you know, because of my mom, but that's all that there is to it." I couldn't bear for him to know how I really felt about Alex. I didn't want him to know how weak I really am.

"Do you like him, Briana?"

"Of course I do. He's a great guy. But I know him well and I know what to expect from him."

"OK. Actually, Alex really is a good guy. If he's smart, then he'll come to understand what a great girl he's got just underneath his nose. And he better not hurt you, otherwise he'll have me to deal with."

Rocco's words were playful, but I knew that he meant them. Never in my life had anyone had my back. I was overcome with emotion. Maybe I wasn't alone anymore. Maybe there finally was someone who cared about and looked out for *me*.

"Ah come on, honey. You're not crying again. Please don't cry."

I put my arms around Rocco's neck and hugged him hard. I wanted to cry. I think I needed to cry. The tears felt good. To my horror, I noticed that I soiled his Canali shirt with my runny nose. Rocco noticed it too. He didn't say anything, although I'm pretty sure that I saw him gag a little.

"Hey, don't I throw great parties! Who needs a funeral when you can come over to my place? Good entertainment, great food, and tears are guaranteed." Rocco spoke into my hair, gently rubbing my back with one hand as I continued to hold on to him. "Baby, I've been too hard on you tonight. I'm sorry. Forgive me."

"Yes, you have been hard on me. But you've also been great. I can feel how much you care about me, Rocco. You know we really are very much alike, you and I."

"You think so, honey?"

"*Oh yeah*. Well, we're both strong and tough—yes, Rocco, I'm tough too. But we're essentially good, in here." I placed my hand on his chest, over his heart. "And we're both so loyal. I don't think that being loyal is necessarily a good thing, you know. Maybe we're too loyal for our own good. It's often not worth it, unfortunately. But Rocco, I care about you too, and I am loyal to you. I've got your back, babe!" I tried to pat him on his shoulder with my hand.

I was feeling a little dizzy and a little nauseous. I was so tired, my arms firmly wrapped around Rocco's neck. He now had his arms just as firmly wrapped around my body, pretty much keeping me on my feet.

Rocco held me back a little, just enough to look at my face. "Honey, how much have you had to drink?"

"Oh, not very much at all."

"And have you eaten anything?"

"Oh, not very much at all." I smiled up at him, and a hiccup escaped my mouth before I could stifle it with my hand. "Oops, sorry."

"Good God, you're drunk!" Rocco's eyes were narrowed, and his mouth was taut.

"Don't be silly. I'm not drunk. I hardly had

anything to drink."

"Yeah, so you said, *not very much at all*."

"Will this night ever end?" Rocco exclaimed in exasperation.

"I *know*. I mean *really*, Rocco. What a night I've had here! First you humiliated me in front of Dr. Ferrante, then I cried and we made up. And get this: I made out with Alex!" I couldn't help giggling. Rocco wasn't amused. "And then you showed me that you care about me, and I cried again! But they were good tears, *you know*?"

"Yeah, I know." Rocco put one arm around me and the other at my knees and he swept me up against his chest. "What are you doing?"

Totally disregarding my question and my dignity, he muttered between his teeth, "Drunk!"

"I can't let you go back in there, Briana, and there's no way that you're driving home in this condition. You're accident prone when you're sober; I shudder to think at what can happen to you when you're drunk."

"But where are you taking me?"

"Upstairs, to my room, away from the other guests. They should be gone soon, and hopefully by then you'll feel better and I'll be able to take you home. Drunk! Really, Briana? It's a good thing that your kids are spending the night at your mom's. I was right. You're like a child who needs to be watched at all times. *Honestly*." Luckily, the way to Rocco's room was in the back of the house and far away from the area where most of the guests were lingering, so I didn't have to be seen by anyone in my "weakened state."

"But I hardly had anything to drink. I should be telling you to put me down, but I like being in your arms." I rested my head on his shoulder. "You're so strong. Such broad shoulders." I let my finger trail over his ear in a light caress. "You have nice ears, Rocco." I was giggling.

He jerked his head away, but he was grinning. "Behave!"

"You're so handsome, you know that?" I reached forward and lightly kissed the scar above his eye. His step faltered for a second. "Don't do that."

When we finally got to his room, he dropped me on his bed. He bent to remove my shoes and told me to lie back and take a nap.

He then sat on the edge of the bed next to me. "Would you like me to bring you something to eat, or some coffee maybe?"

"Oh, no thanks. I'm a little nauseous."

Rocco got up briefly and returned with a bath towel from his en suite bathroom. "Just in case you need it. My guests should be gone soon. I'll be back to check on you in a little while, OK?"

"OK, don't worry about me. I'll be just fine up here in your big, comfy bed." I grabbed a pillow and hugged it close to me. "I'll pretend that this here pillow is you. OK, Rocco? Just until you get back to me. Then I'd like very much to get back into your arms. *Into your strong arms.*" I drifted off to sleep.

By the time Rocco made his way back to his guests, some were finally beginning to leave. Dr. Ferrante was a little surprised and disappointed to learn, from Rocco, that Briana had to leave unexpectedly due to a headache. Rocco wasn't about to tell Alex that Briana was upstairs, tucked away in his bed. He knew that if Alex was aware that Briana wasn't feeling well, then he would be his usual *upstanding* self, play the *hero*, and take care of her, *right here in Rocco's home.* He wasn't about to let Alex score such easy points. *Let Alex work for Briana's affection!* And besides, Briana didn't need Alex's help. Rocco was perfectly capable of making sure that she was alright.

The last guests had left, and Rocco was able to return to his room. Briana was asleep, still hugging her pillow. He stood at the foot of the bed and watched her sleep for a while. She was beautiful. She was smart and strong. But what a little disaster she was! She needed a good, strong man in her life. Someone that would help her raise her children and look out for her and keep her from hurting herself. "I don't know if Alex is strong enough to be your man," he whispered to himself as he looked down at Briana. Rocco decided that he would change and sleep in one of the guest bedrooms. He would let Briana sleep in his bed tonight. He never let any of his women sleep in his bed. He always used one of the guest bedrooms when he *entertained*. But this was different. Briana wasn't one of his women.

Rocco changed into pajama bottoms. He usually just slept in his underwear. He was about to leave the room but then decided that he should first remove Briana's dress. It was a pretty dress that would be ruined in the morning if she slept in it all night long. He would leave her in her bra and panties.

He knew that Briana was pretty, but he didn't realize just how pretty until he saw her lying on his bed, with practically nothing on. *She was perfect,* he thought. Her breasts were big enough to make them enticing, but not big enough to give the impression of vulgarity. Her waist was small and her hips curvaceous, with a nicely rounded ass. She was petite, but her legs were long and shapely. She was definitely the type of woman that you kissed, on the face. She was a sweetheart. Even her kisses were sweet. He remembered how sweet her lips felt to him when he kissed her that day in his office. And her touch was so gentle. She had kissed him again today. But she was drunk and didn't really understand what she was doing. Good thing, because he wasn't about to fall for someone again, and well, Briana wasn't the type to just fuck around with.

Briana suddenly moved, shifting her position in the bed. The soft light from the lamp on the night table was still on. She reached up with her hand to rub her eyes, then looked up at Rocco and smiled shyly at him. "Dr. Ferrante." Her voice was low and husky. Rocco's mouth tightened in anger. *What a little fool,* he thought. She really did have a thing for the good doctor.

"Oh, Rocco. It's you. You came back."

Rocco sat next to her on the bed. He reached forward to brush some hair away from her face. "How are you feeling, honey?" Despite still feeling angry, his voice was soft and his touch tender on her face.

"I'm good, and so tired." She giggled and grabbed Rocco's hand just as he was going to remove it from where he had it placed on her cheek. She was obviously still under the influence.

Rocco got up and slowly began to walk toward the door. "Briana, I'm going to be in the bedroom down the hall if you need me OK."

"Oh no, don't leave me, Rocco. Please, stay with me. I want to fall asleep in your strong arms. I feel so safe with you, you know? *It feels so good.* Come on, *honey.*" She patted the mattress next to her and let out a soft, sensual laugh.

Rocco was going to leave, but her laugh was infectious and it kept him rooted to where he was standing. He looked at her lying there, looking beautiful, so soft and inviting. She needed him, and he never could resist a damsel in distress.

"Do you realize what you're asking of me?"

"Oh, don't be silly, Rocco. I'm not asking you to *make love to me,* you know. I just want you to sleep with me, OK. So come over here already so I can cuddle up to your strong, virile body and get some sleep. I'm so tired." She yawned and giggled again.

"Oh, what the hell." Rocco went to turn off the light before getting into bed.

"Geez, Rocco. Look at you. You're awesome! You're, like, photoshopped or something." Briana was referring to his perfectly sculpted torso, her eyes opened wide in appreciation.

He grinned down at her and gathered her into his arms. She snuggled in closer to him and rubbed her nose in his chest. Her even, steady breathing finally told him that she was fast asleep.

He couldn't believe what he was doing. He was breaking all of his rules. But this probably didn't count, as Briana wasn't one of his women. She felt so good in his arms. He grinned, feeling like he was sleeping with a little doll. She was a doll, a fragile one, and he would protect her. She shifted her position, causing his hand to sit right on top of her behind. He could feel the smooth skin underneath his hand and the full roundness of her perfect little ass. He was a man, after all, and there was no way that he could control the reaction that she was causing his body to have. But this wasn't just any girl. So he resigned himself to being sexually frustrated, at least just for this one night, and gathered her up closer into his arms. He tilted her head up to him and, with a sigh, he kissed her gently on her forehead, nose, and mouth. "Sleep good, baby," he whispered into her hair. Yeah, she was his sweet little disaster.

I woke up the next morning with a throbbing headache, and feeling a little confused. When I finally realized where I was, I gasped in horror. I was in Rocco's bed, in my bra and panties! And where was Rocco? I started to remember all of the events of the previous evening. Sure, I was a little emotional, but I had been provoked. There's only so much that I can handle nowadays. Ever since my divorce, and after my incredibly bad marriage filled with pain and abuse, I have such a low tolerance for any type of verbal abuse.

And my kids? Thank goodness that they were safe and sound at my mom's.

I made out with Dr. Ferrante! I couldn't help but laugh as I thought about how we kissed like a couple of teenagers on the bench in Rocco's backyard. He was crazy if he thought that I would agree to a casual, part-time, "whenever the mood should strike" type of relationship with him. But God, I sure did want to be with him, sexually, and there really was no denying it.

And how about that Rocco? He could be so abrasive, and yet so gentle and tender. If he ever does fall in love again, then that woman will definitely be one lucky person. Rocco would be a good, strong, caring and loving husband. But he probably won't ever let himself love again. And there's no doubt in my mind that he'd be an excellent lover. I shamelessly clung to him last night. I don't know why I acted that way with him, but I do know that I just needed him. It felt so damn good to be in his arms. Although I was unable to keep my eyes open while in his arms, I could definitely feel him touching me. He must've thought that I was asleep, but I wasn't. His touch was light but thorough. I felt like he was trying to feel every part of my body. It was a little startling for me to feel my body tingle with pleasure at his touch. Maybe it was because of the alcohol that I had consumed. *Just two glasses of wine!* And there was no denying the effect that it was having on Rocco either. I could feel his huge bulge rub up against my belly. Gosh! They say that size doesn't matter, but what a delight to be with a man who is so well endowed. The possibilities were endless, and it made me blush to realize how excited a man could get me. I needed to get laid, and it was starting to get to me!

So I got up and realized that Rocco must be downstairs as it was already after 10 a.m. . I quickly put on a pajama top that was neatly folded on the bench at the end of the bed, and I made my way downstairs. It was a black silk pajama shirt. *How typically Rocco.* I could hear Dean Martin's "You're Nobody till Somebody Loves You" coming from the kitchen. Rocco was sitting at the table on his terrace off of the kitchen. He had a mug of steaming coffee in front of him and was reading the paper.

"Well hello there, *lover*. Sleep OK?" He was grinning, and his look was mocking. He was wearing the black silk pajama bottoms.

"Shut up, Rocco." I sat on the chair across from him at the table. "Next time you throw a party, don't invite me, OK?"

"It's not my fault if you don't know how to behave, or if you don't know how to handle your liquor." His tone was playful.

"Breakfast will be ready in a few minutes." He got up and headed inside. "Just sit right back down and be a nice little guest," he called out as I got up to follow him.

Rocco was cooking eggs and bacon. At a certain point he just looked at me and I thought that I saw a strange look cross over his eyes. "What?" I asked, feeling a little embarrassed. I looked awful, and I hadn't even combed my hair. I ran my hand through my hair and tried to put some order into it.

"No, don't do that. You look exactly the way that you should look right now. *The way one looks after spending a night in her lover's arms.*" He was being sarcastic and playful, again and he was succeeding in embarrassing me. "But seriously, you look good in my clothes, Briana. Maybe you should wear them more often."

The eggs were delicious, and I was starving. "Thanks, Rocco, for breakfast. And for *everything*."

I couldn't even look into his eyes as I was thanking him for the intimacy that we had shared and the affection that he had shown me last night.

"Don't mention it, darling."

Rocco turned to get himself another cup of coffee. He thought about how good Briana looked to him this morning. Her hair was a tangled mess, she was barefoot, and even the huge shirt that she was wearing couldn't cover up the perfection of her slender body. He needed to get her out of his home, far away from him, and fast. She was beginning to get another *rise* out of him this morning, and this time there wasn't the excuse of too much alcohol that would keep him honorable and noble.

18

Dr. Alex Ferrante

"**I** know that you're feeling a little anxious, and it's perfectly normal. Just think, after this you'll be able to do all of the things that you've always wanted to do but couldn't." Dr. Ferrante leaned forward and kissed his patient on the forehead. "I'll be there with you the whole time."

His patient, Melissa, was a sweet woman of only twenty-four years old. She was being prepped for lung transplant surgery. Dr. Ferrante loved being in surgery, and this type of surgery was by far his favorite. He was at peace in the operating room, where he could be free to do what he knows best and what he truly loves to do without any interruptions. Still, he could appreciate his patient's anxiety and fear. It's scary as hell to know that you'll be waking up with someone else's lungs inside of you. *Someone who had to die in order to give you a second chance at life.* Feeling a little guilty was a natural reaction that many of his patients expressed, and it was totally understandable.

The doctor was just about ready to begin. All he needed to do was go through his ritual of saying a small prayer before beginning his work. It helped him focus on shutting his mind to anything other than the task at hand. Although he is a man of science, he is certainly wise enough to understand that there has to be a higher power out there. So he thought of his prayer as a little back-up plan. After all, he owed it to his patients to be open and accepting of all options.

Over eight hours later, the doctor was back in his office, finishing off his report before heading out. The operation was a success, so it had been a good day.

"Dr. Ferrante, can I get you something? How about some coffee, or something to eat, or anything else that you might like?" The pretty little nurse was looking at the doctor with open admiration in her eyes. He clearly understood that she was offering him more than just coffee. *She certainly is a looker*, he thought. God, he could hardly look away from the straining buttons of her shirt. She was stacked, alright, and she knew how to use it to her advantage. Yeah, sure, there was something that she could get him. But he never fucked around with anybody at work. He took his job way too seriously to ever allow anything to compromise the integrity of his work or tarnish his golden reputation. "It's real kind of you to ask, but no thank you. I'm good."

"Alright, Doctor, but if you decide that you need anything at all, my shift ends in a half hour. By the way, congratulations on your surgery today."

He was headed home when he realized that he had that *thing* tonight. *Is the official opening of Tommy's restaurant tonight?* he wondered. Yeah, it was, but he just wanted to get home. He had promised that he would attend, and Tommy was his cousin, so he figured he should go by and have a quick bite before heading for home.

"Alex, you finally made it! Come with me. I'll show you around the restaurant," Tommy said with pride in his voice. Alex had to admit that the newly renovated restaurant looked great. For a little man who wouldn't exactly be described by anyone as good-looking, and who obviously didn't have any fashion sense at all, he sure did know how to turn a restaurant around. The restaurant was elegantly decorated, stylish and hip. It would no doubt become one of the new trendy hot spots for affluent Montrealers. Tommy was thrilled that Alex had come to his official opening. After all, the doctor was well known and respected. He was a local celebrity, and his appearance would certainly help the image that Tommy so desperately hoped to achieve for his restaurant.

Alex was feeling exhausted. He had had a good day, but he was ready for it to come to an end already. There was a good turnout at the restaurant, including several members of Alex's family. He was finally having a bite to eat, seated at a table with his brother Carlo, an aunt and uncle, and three of his cousins. Feeling bored, Alex was desperately trying to look interested and to be somewhat sociable. His brother was babbling on about something and he was practically shouting in his ear so that he could be heard over all of the noise and music in the place.

"So, what do you think, Alex? Are you interested?" A financial wiz, Carlo was the CFO of a very big corporation. He wanted Alex to invest in a personal project that Carlo promised would bring in thousands of dollars. Alex didn't need the money, as he had enough to keep him living in a very comfortable lifestyle, but he certainly wasn't opposed to making even more money. "Sure, Carlo, just send me the information and I'll look through it as soon as I get a chance." Alex trusted Carlo's business sense, but above all he trusted his own. He would never agree to anything without conducting due diligence of his own.

There were plenty of beautiful women in the place. Carlo leaned over and discreetly gestured toward the gorgeous restaurant hostess standing next to the bar. "She hasn't stopped looking at you, Alex. She really wants you, that's for sure." Alex knew exactly who Carlo was referring to, as he had noticed her immediately upon entering the restaurant. Wherever he went, there was a beautiful girl just waiting to be with the great doctor and openly throwing herself at him. Alex just shrugged his shoulders, feeling more bored than ever.

Soon afterwards, the hostess came by with a bottle of wine. She poured the wine for all of them at the table and then lingered by Alex's chair. He could smell her perfume. Yeah, she was hot, alright. She was looking at him with those dark almond-shaped eyes, which were set against her dark skin and long black hair. She was an exotic beauty. She leaned over to him, with her ample bosom brushing against him, and looked at him straight in the eyes. She was standing so close to him that he could feel her breath on his cheek. Alex focused on her full, sensual mouth, as she asked him for a favor. "Dr. Ferrante, Tommy tells me that you are quite the wine connoisseur. Would you kindly come down with me into the wine cellar to help me pick out a wine for a special dish that the chef is thinking of adding to the menu?"

Really? She needs help picking out a wine? He had already turned down a fine piece of ass earlier today, so maybe he should just go help out the poor thing already. *I am a doctor, after all, and it's my job to help people. Hell, I took an oath!* For a moment he thought about how nice it would be if it wasn't just so damn easy. Women were just so eager nowadays, and it took some of the fun out of it. But her full lips held a promise of sensual softness. They did look like they would wrap themselves easily around his prick, which was getting harder by the minute. "It would be my pleasure to assist you, umm..." he got up and couldn't finish his sentence as he realized that he didn't know her name."

"My name is Gisele. Please follow me."

And Alex did, down to the wine cellar, away from all of the guests.

They sure didn't waste any time when they got to the cellar. Gisele's mouth was wrapped around Alex's cock, and she was sucking him hard. Although it felt just as good as he had imagined that it would, after a few minutes he was beginning to lose interest and he could feel his hard-on softening. He pulled her up close to him, wanting to feel her wet pussy. That always could get him back in the mood. *Oh but how he loved the feel of pussy. Oh but how he wished he could find a woman who would just say no.* Instinct took his finger to the magic spot, and he knew that he'd found it when she let out a deep groan. Gisele handed him a condom. So, she had prepared for this. *What a turn off*, he thought, but still better to be safe than sorry. He inserted his prick inside her and began to screw her, increasing his stroke, wishing that it would be over quickly. Within seconds he felt her climax. He withdrew and pulled up his pants.

He smiled at Gisele and turned to head for the stairs. "That was great. Thanks."

"Oh no, Dr. Ferrante, thank *you*. Will I see you again?"

"Yeah, sure. I'll be coming by." He looked back at her with that sexy smile of his. He felt like shit.

Alex made his way back to the table, feeling a little empty and disappointed, and announced that he needed to leave because he had an early-morning run the next day. His brother Carlo threw him a questioning look, to which Alex replied with a grin, "I struck out."

"You fucking liar," Carlo returned with a grin of his own.

Shortly after, Dr. Ferrante was finally on his way home. He drove by the Foundation's office, as it was on the way to his home. He wondered if Briana was working there tonight. Probably not, as it was pretty late and Briana was surely at home caring for her children. He hadn't seen her since Rocco's party. She had left the party without saying goodbye to him. He knew that it was probably because of his offer of a casual sexual relationship. He didn't understand how or why he had made the offer in the first place. He absolutely knew that she would not agree to it. She was too wholesome. But after that night in the office, well, *best damn hard-on that he had ever had*! He was indeed a little drunk, but he knew exactly what he was doing, and he had wanted her badly. She tasted so good, and she made the sexiest little sounds when he touched her. There was a lot of passion buried deep inside of her, and he wanted her to unleash it all over him. And then they made out at Rocco's party. They made out like a couple of kids! She made him feel like a teenager with raging hormones and it was just so refreshing to be with her.

Still, he knew that Briana had a thing for him. He had known from the very beginning. And he had always thought of her as sexy, kind, and smart. But he understood the type of woman that she was. Briana was too emotionally involved to ever agree to simply having a casual sexual relationship with him. He also knew how easy it was for him to get her to give in to her passion once he had her in his arms. She seemed to melt in his arms. The look of complete trust in her eyes as she looked at him made him feel so guilty. Maybe that was why he offered her a casual sexual relationship. God knows it was a hell of a lot more than what he'd offered any other woman since his divorce.

Finally home, he headed straight for bed. He was about to turn off the lights when he got an idea that made him smile to himself. He took his phone as he was going to text Briana. "Just like the old days." He couldn't help but laugh.

"Hey there...are you asleep?"

He waited for a response.
Almost immediately, Briana responded.

"Hi. I never sleep. What are you doing up so late?"

"My thoughts are keeping me awake."

"Erotic thoughts, are they?"

"Yes, and they're all of you."

No response from Briana. Alex waited, and still no response.

"Briana?"

"What?"

"Where's the nasty comeback that I was expecting from you?"

"Nasty? Moi? When have I ever been nasty to you? Go to sleep, Alex."

"You're right, you're not nasty. You're witty, but you do have a smart little mouth."

"Get some rest, Doctor, otherwise you may find yourself ripping out the wrong vital organs tomorrow in surgery! Goodnight."

"If you had accepted my offer, then you'd be with me now, and then I'd surely have a good night. Hope I don't accidentally remove someone's aorta tomorrow...Sweet dreams."

Briana had a way of always making him feel good. He enjoyed the playful banter between the two of them. He thought about how kind she was, and selfless. She stayed on his mind until he drifted off to sleep.

"Has there been any change, Mrs. Laurent?" Alex asked the live-in caregiver who was looking after Claire, his ex-wife." He couldn't help but ask, even though he always received the same response."

"No, sir. None at all," Mrs. Laurent said sympathetically. She seemed to feel sorry for Alex, who was Claire's only visitor.

"Please, Mrs. Laurent, go ahead and take a break. I'll be here for a little while."

Claire was sitting in her usual spot, in a rocking chair facing the window. Dr. Ferrante pulled up a chair and sat down beside her. "Doesn't the sun feel good, Claire?" It was a beautiful sunny day, and the whole room was filled with the warmth of the sun bursting in through the huge windows. "You always loved to sunbathe, even though I always told you that it would give you wrinkles prematurely." Dr. Ferrante smiled, and simply sighed at the lost look on Claire's face. *Why is she like this?* he thought. What caused her to be trapped inside of her mind and body, unable to speak, or react, or really live? Dr. Ferrante reached out and gently moved some of her mousy brown hair away from her face.

Alex met Claire during his first year of residency. Claire worked as a nurse in the same hospital as Alex. It wasn't exactly love at first sight for Alex, as Claire wasn't even the type of girl that usually sparked his interest. However, she was a pretty young woman and she was outgoing and attractive. She had set her mind on getting Alex from the very first day that she had seen him. After a couple of years of dating, Claire demanded a real commitment from Alex, so he agreed to marry her. Alex did love Claire, but he never really felt that passionate, romantic love that you read about in a book or a poem, or that you see on the big screen at the movies. They had a comfortable love. A man of science, Alex was very practical. He fully understood that all that was required in a good marriage was love, friendship, and respect for one another. The passionate love that so many people desired would pretty much serve to disappoint once it would fade, as it surely would, and the loss would eventually hurt the relationship. Still, Alex had been a faithful husband to Claire, and she had betrayed him. He had been hurt and betrayed, but it had been surprisingly easy for him to leave Claire and ask for a divorce. There had been no real passion in his relationship with Claire, and none to speak of in their marriage, and even the divorce was passionless. It was quick and amicable.

As Alex looked at Claire—lost, motionless, lifeless—all he could feel was pity for this woman. He wanted to help her. He wished that she would get better and live a normal life again. He placed his hand on Claire's and rubbed it, hoping that she would feel the physical human contact. She wasn't alone. He hoped that she understood that. Alex then reached for the book that was left open on the table next to Claire's chair. "OK, Claire, how about we do a little reading?" And he began to read out loud, softly, the story about the firefighter from Precinct #8 who had risked his life to save a puppy from a burning inferno.

After the divorce, Alex decided that he would never marry again. He felt that he obviously wasn't very good at being married, so why would he ever set himself up to fail again? No, he wouldn't go through that again. And he couldn't love just one woman; he loved them all. There were just too many beautiful women out there to ever be able to pick just one. The women just seemed to flock to him. And he enjoyed himself immensely. Dr. Ferrante was hardworking and devoted to helping his patients, and he enjoyed the simple pleasures in life. It was a good balance. Still, he couldn't help but feel that something was missing in his life. There was indeed a void and he felt it, but he couldn't quite put his finger on it. But then again he always did feel like something was missing. At first he thought that his success as a surgeon would fill that void, but it didn't, although his greatest satisfaction did come through his work. Maybe he just expected too much out of life, or needed too much. Whatever the reason, apart from when he was in the operating room, he always seemed to feel a little bored. He was used to it by now, and he just learned to live with it.

Dr. Ferrante had just arrived home from the hospital. It had been a good day, but so exhausting. A quick bite and an early night was what he had in mind for this evening.

Who the heck could that be at this time of night? His doorbell was ringing. "Hold on!" he bellowed as the doorbell shrieked impatiently.

"Briana, what are you doing here?" Dr. Ferrante was obviously surprised to see Briana, although he was also excited to see her. "Excuse me, please come in."

"Hello there. Hope I'm not interrupting."

"Not at all. Please sit down and make yourself comfortable. What can I get you? Maybe some wine?"

"I'm good, thanks. Please, just come sit down. I need to speak to you."

"Sure, sweetheart. What is it?"

"You know how I feel about you. Although I've been denying it, it's absolutely true. Alex, I'm so attracted to you. You're all I think about. I can't take it anymore! I'm so tired of fighting this. I want you, body and soul, and I want you to take me, right now."

Alex sat across from Briana, both stunned and delighted. "I knew you'd come around." He watched in amazement as Briana got up and began to undo the buttons of her coat. All she was wearing underneath was pearl-colored lace. Her bra was lacy and low-cut, with a matching lace thong panty and garter belt. She was a vision of beauty, and Alex couldn't help but feel that this was what a woman should be wearing on her wedding night. The perfect gift for any husband.

Briana approached Alex and lifted one leg up onto the chair where he was seated. "Do you like what you see, Alex? I can see that you do." She reached down with one hand and stroked his bulging manhood through his pants. "Make love to me, Alex. Show me that you want me. I need you to take me now."

Alex had to remind himself to breathe, as he felt like he must be in some hypnotic trance. He was completely mesmerized by her powers of seduction. She turned a little away from him so she could begin to undress. She undid her bra, allowing her ample breasts to spill out, just inviting him to reach for them with his hands. She undid the clips of her garter and turned her back to Alex. She lightly ran her hands over her perfect round ass, and it was all that he could do to keep from grabbing it and biting into the tender flesh.

Once she was completely undressed, she

turned to face him once again.

Alex found the strength to come back from his altered state of consciousness. Briana stood in front of him, in all her beautiful naked glory, with a deep hunger in her eyes. He realized that she was hungry, alright. *Hungry for him*. Alex rose from his seat and pulled Briana up against his chest. He reached back and grabbed her ass with his hands, pulling her even closer to him. Then he kissed her on the lips. He brushed his lips against hers, lightly and gently. With a deep groan, he picked her up into his arms and headed for his bedroom.

He looked into her smoldering eyes. "I am going to make love to you, Briana. I will make you mine, and you will never want for another again." Alex kissed Briana's neck, her shoulders, her belly and her legs. Although his need was urgent, he desired to show her that he not only wanted to take her but he needed to make love to every beautiful inch of her body.

"*What the fuck!*" Alex was having another one of his dreams again. This had kept happening to him ever since that day at the Foundation, when he met Briana. He was frustrated because he never did get the job done, as far as Briana was concerned. But this was ridiculous! He was acting like a teenager with raging hormones, waking up after having a wet dream. He laughed a little to himself. "Yeah, she makes me feel like a kid again!" But Alex was no teen. He was a respected surgeon, and he could have his pick of any woman, any night of the week.

And having these recurring dreams didn't even bother him as much as the *tone* of the dreams. He could understand dreaming about having sex with a woman. But this wasn't really *sex* that he was dreaming about. He wanted to *make love* to Briana. He wanted to possess her, love her. *What the fuck is the matter with me?* he wondered. He needed to do something about this. And he would think about doing just that, after a much-needed cold shower.

Alex emerged from the shower feeling more relaxed and a little playful. He wasn't sure that he liked the way things were going as far as his thoughts and desires went with the whole Briana situation. But he knew that it didn't feel entirely bad. He was laughing a little more nowadays. He even felt a little silly! He couldn't believe that he, a respected and sought-after surgeon, could feel this way. "I mean, really? I'm the 'Wayne Gretzky of pulmonary medicine,' aren't I?" He said this in a playful, sarcastic tone. Still, how refreshing to find a woman who didn't fall at his feet. "That must be it," he whispered to himself.

He wanted to speak to Briana. He needed to see her. He reached for his cell phone as he decided that texting her was always the s*afest* way to approach her.

> *"Hi, Briana. Have dinner with me on Thursday evening?"*

Sweet and to the point.

Alex waited for her response, and as usual he didn't have to wait long to receive it.

> *"No."*

That was it.

> *"Why not? I want to try out a new restaurant, and I'm sure that the food will taste great if you'll be there to share it with me. I promise that I'll be on my best behavior. And besides, I need to discuss some fundraising options with you."*

> *"Alex, I already have plans."*

> *"Who with? Cancel them."*

> *"NO."*

> *"Briana, you will have dinner with me on Thursday. I'll pick you up at 7 p.m."*

> *"NO. I'm turning off my phone now."*

"What the hell is the matter with this woman? Alex wondered. *She has given me every reason to believe that she is into me, since the very beginning. And now that I actually want to see her, she's playing these little games with me. And who did she have plans with on Thursday? Was she seeing another guy? No, no, she will have dinner with*

me, not some other guy! Alex was feeling a little snubbed, a little confused, and a whole lot frustrated. He picked up his phone, searched for her home number, and dialed it.

"Hello?" Briana responded after two rings. If she hadn't responded so quickly, he would have had no choice but to go over to her place and talk some sense into her, in person.

"Have dinner with me on Thursday."

"Oh, for the love of God! What is it with you? Can't take *NO* for an answer?"

"Who are you meeting on Thursday, Briana? Who is he? Is it Rocco?"

"OK, Alex. I don't owe you any explanations, but if you must know, I'm taking my kids to Place des Arts on Thursday to watch a show. And just so we understand each other, it's NONE of your BUSINESS who I see or decide to have dinner with! Got it? Understand? *Hai Capito?*"

Alex sighed in relief. "You know, you could've just said so, sweetheart."

"Are you for real? Who do you think you are telling me what to do? We're not at the hospital, Dr. Ferrante, and YOU are not the boss of ME!"

"OK, take it easy. I didn't mean to come across as being so bossy. I'm sorry, sweetheart. I would really love to have dinner with you, on a night other than Thursday, whenever it's good for you. Whenever, wherever, just so long as I can see you soon."

"I don't know if that's such a good idea, given

what has already happened between us."

"Come on now, nothing really happened. We shared a few kisses, I offered you a proposition, and you shut me down. I like having you as a friend, and I'd like to see you. Besides, I need to speak to you about some fundraising that we need to arrange. If my dashing good looks and charming personality aren't enough to immediately draw you to me, then *do it for the Foundation*."

"Real smooth, Doctor. OK, I can be available on Friday."

"Good girl! I'll pick you up at 7 p.m., at your home. And Briana?"

"Yes?"

"I look forward to seeing you on Friday. Good night, sweetheart."

"Good night."

19

Do I Talk Slow?

It was Friday afternoon, and it had been a long week. I had difficulty writing my column, as I just couldn't concentrate. Alex had been on my mind, of course. I'd had a taste of what it was like to make love with him, and I think that it was just a little too much for me. His mouth was sensual and strong, and his kisses were delicious and intoxicating. I was, however, a little surprised at how forceful he was. Oh, there is no doubt in my mind that he is kind and that he has a gentle heart. But he's not exactly sweet. He is a little arrogant and demanding, and he doesn't sugarcoat anything. He's direct and to the point. Most men, except for Peter, of course, have always treated me like I am fragile and need to be handled delicately. Peter always treated me in a pretty shitty way. Although Alex doesn't treat me as if I'm fragile, he's not shitty with me either. He's forceful but not hurtful, at least not physically, and he seems to take what he wants. He kisses me, and he grabs hold of me, and he holds me tight to him. Is it sick that I find it a little sexy?

Even my session with Rocco was a little difficult today. I just couldn't concentrate, and Rocco seemed to be a little impatient with me. What I also found a little surprising was that I think I caught him *checking me out* a couple of times. I'm pretty sure that he was looking at my ass when I got up to get myself a drink. It felt a little strange, but at the same time I couldn't help but wonder if I looked good to him. Did he think me attractive? Could a man like Rocco, someone so virile and masculine, find someone like me attractive? And then I thought about how the two men that are in my life right now are so different from one another. Alex is my dream man, he is my fantasy. He is a respected surgeon. One expects a doctor to be gentle and *soft* somehow, but Alex isn't *soft* at all. On the contrary, he is actually a little *hard*, although he does indeed have a gentle heart. And Rocco, well, Rocco is the opposite. Rocco is my friend. His looming presence, the broadness of his shoulders, even his name all seem to suggest that he is rough and maybe even a little tough. However, you couldn't find a gentler giant than Rocco.

Both men seem to have their fair share of baggage, as it seems that they are constantly struggling with issues and their own personal demons. But then again, who doesn't have their fair share of baggage in life? God knows I have so much of it.

Rocco was rubbing the scar above his eye with his thumb. "OK, Rocco, what's up with you today? You seem as though you want to say something to me. So just say it."

"Have you seen Alex lately, Briana?"

"No," I said, although I had been in contact with him, and I was having dinner with him tonight. But Rocco didn't need to know this information.

"You love him, don't you?"

"Don't be ridiculous, Rocco!"

"Briana, do I talk slow? Do you think that I'm stupid? It's obvious that you care about him. I do think that you need a man, but I'm not sure that Alex is the one for you."

"I don't need a man."

"Yeah, every woman needs a man. And you, Briana, are especially in need of a man."

"Rocco, a woman doesn't need a man. All a woman *does* need, however, is a good set of batteries." I giggled to myself as I wondered if Rocco understood the meaning behind my last comment.

"You see, Briana, that's why I say that you need a man in your life. You mention needing a *vibrator*, talking as if you're so experienced, and then you giggle and blush like a young schoolgirl.

I bet you've never even seen a vibrator, let alone ever used one. The only batteries that you need are for the remote control of your television!"

Rocco never ceases to amaze me. It's like he can read my mind! And I only *giggled* because it was a funny joke. I'm sure Alex would've appreciated my *witty* joke. Although Rocco was fuckin' right in saying that I had never even seen a vibrator before in my life. Fuckin' Rocco!

"You need a man that will look after you and keep you from hurting yourself. *God, Briana.* I can see what you find so appealing about Alex, but a lot of women find the same things appealing about him. And he loves women. I don't know if he can love just one woman. You need a man that will be a good husband to you and a good father to your children."

"OK, easy now, Rocco. Husband? A good father to my children? We're getting a little ahead of ourselves, aren't we now? I don't want a husband. My children have *me.* I work hard to give them everything that they do need, and they don't need an asshole in their lives fucking it all up. And stop acting like my father! You don't seem to be looking for a woman that's *wife material.* Maybe I just want the same things that you want, Rocco. Maybe I just want a man for the same reasons that you just want a woman."

"Now you're just disgusting me, Briana, so knock it off. You're not like that, and I don't want to hear you say such things." Rocco's eyes were dark and furious, and his mouth was tightened in anger.

Like hell I 'wasn't like that.' I needed to be with a man just as much as he needed to be with a woman. Possibly more so as I hadn't gotten any in so damn long.

This conversation was ridiculous, and I just wanted to lighten things between me and Rocco. "Look, Rocco, I just want to take care of my kids, do my work, and have a little fun if it's possible. I really appreciate that you're being a good friend and all, looking out for me. But I'm not stupid either, Rocco." *Well, maybe just a little.* "I have a date tonight, so maybe I *will* find a good husband really soon."

"A date?" Rocco, looking a little surprised, cocked his head to one side. "Huh. Who with?"

"Nobody you know, Rocco. He's someone that I met at church last Sunday. He's some kind of a mechanic. Yeah, that's it, he fixes things. We're just going out for an early dinner. And now, please, no more talk about this, OK? Let's try to finish our work quickly so I can go home and get ready for my big date."

Rocco was quiet for the remainder of our time together. He continued to rub his scar though, and that's never a good thing. I lied to him about having a date with a mechanic. I just wanted him to get off my back already, and I knew that he wouldn't like the idea of my dating Alex. Rocco was acting a little possessive lately, and I didn't quite know how to handle it, really. We had shared some intimate moments, and so maybe that's what was making him act in this way. I could sense that Rocco was also a little disconcerted by his own behavior toward me. His feelings about me were obviously ambivalent. I could see this through the many different expressions that crossed his face as he silently watched me. I have to admit that I too had felt a little different about Rocco ever since I used him as my human teddy bear the other night in his home. I really enjoyed falling asleep in Rocco's arms. I felt so safe in his big, strong arms. His hands are huge and yet so gentle. *He* is so gentle. And yet he is so masculine. If he wasn't my friend, and if I was the type of person who could simply have sex with a man, then I do believe that I would truly enjoy having sex with Rocco. I do believe that it would be wild.

20

Oh Yeah, He's a Smooth Operator...

It was quickly approaching 7 p.m., and Alex would be here to pick me up at any minute. I didn't want to look like I was all dressed up for a date, as Alex did say that he wanted to discuss some fundraising options with me. I decided on a little black dress as I figured that I really couldn't go wrong with it.

Alex was five minutes early. Dressed in black dress pants and a light-blue shirt, he showed up at my front door with a beautiful bouquet of flowers. He always managed to take my breath away.

He looked at me with that lazy, sexy smile of his. "Hi, beautiful." He handed me the flowers and stepped inside, without waiting for me to invite him in. As I reached for the flowers, he bent down a little and gave me a quick kiss on the mouth.

"Alex, come in," I said a little sarcastically. "You shouldn't have bothered, although they are beautiful. Thank you." In reality, I love flowers. I couldn't remember the last time that anyone gave me flowers. It felt nice.

"*You* are beautiful, Briana. And you smell nice too." Alex reached forward and hugged me to him. He buried his face in my neck and ran one hand through my hair. "You're delicious, sweetheart."

I wanted to die in his arms, but instead I pushed him away. "Alex, stop that."

"Right! Where are the kids?" He must have thought that the risk of Marco and Elisa running into us and catching us in an embrace was the reason for my pushing him away.

"My kids aren't here. They're at a sleepover at a friend's house." I really didn't want my kids to learn that I was actually going on a date with anyone. Why confuse them? There was a mischievous gleam in Alex's eyes. "Let's go, Alex, before it gets too late." I grabbed my purse and headed for the door.

The restaurant was beautiful, and we were given a table on the outdoor terrace. Alex had told me that he loved to eat *al fresco*. So did I. The more we spoke, well, the more I realized just how much

Alex and I had in common. We loved the same things. We had the same taste in music, books, and movies, and we both loved to eat. I didn't tell him that I was a romance novel junky. He could go on thinking that I read the *New England Journal of Medicine*!

I was truly enjoying the spicy beef in sa-tei sauce and the seafood fried noodles, when I noticed that Alex was looking at me with a big grin on his face. I wiped my mouth with my napkin, feeling a little self-conscious. "What? Do I have food stuck in my teeth?" I tried to sound playful, but I could feel the heat creep up my neck under his scrutiny.

"No. I'm just glad to see that you have a good appetite. I can't tell you how annoying it is to sit with a woman who just picks at her food and then claims to be *so full*."

"Well this is just so delicious, Alex. Thank you for taking me here."

"You're welcome. And thank you for coming." I looked at him as the grin on his face turned into his trademark sexy smile. I couldn't help but feel that I wanted to taste his mouth. Would I taste the spicy sauce from the food on his hot, sexy lips? God, he really was too hot for his own good!

And then the couple being led to their table by the waiter caught my attention. I couldn't see the man's face, but those broad, strong shoulders could only belong to Rocco. They were seated at a table at the other end of the terrace, and I hoped that he wouldn't notice Alex and me. As if sensing our presence, Rocco turned his face in our direction and immediately our eyes locked. He looked genuinely surprised to see us there, and then his mouth tightened in a straight line. He turned to say something to his date, and then he got up and made his way to our table.

"Alex, Rocco is coming." For some reason, it sounded like a warning.

"Good evening." Rocco had a smile on his face that didn't quite reach his eyes. He loomed over us, and I felt like we were suddenly caught under a dark storm cloud.

"Hey, Rocco. So nice to see you. Just getting here?" Alex was as cool as a cucumber.

"Yes. Enjoyed your dinner?"

"Yes," Alex and I responded at the same time. To say that it was awkward is an understatement.

"Oh, by the way, Briana, you mentioned something about knowing a really good mechanic today. I'm having some trouble with my car. Would you provide me with the contact information for that mechanic?" Rocco shot a challenging stare my way.

"Sure, Rocco. I'll text you the information later on." I looked at him with the same challenging look that he gave me.

Alex asked Rocco if he wanted to join us for a drink, as we were already done eating our meal.

Rocco declined, stating that he was too hungry and wanted to order his food right away. "OK, well, I don't want to keep my friend waiting by herself for too long. Enjoy the rest of your evening." Rocco nodded to us and walked back to his table. Boy, Rocco could sure pick them. The woman that he was with was gorgeous. She was so sexy. How could I possibly have thought that maybe Rocco could find *me* attractive? I felt so plain and simple.

"Don't bother with them, Briana. You're with me tonight," Alex said with that sexy smile on his face as he reached forward for my hand. He rubbed my hand with his thumb and then let his finger lightly brush over my arm. I shivered at his caressing touch. But my eyes went back to Rocco's table. I guess I was feeling a little guilty for lying to Rocco about my date tonight. Well, it was really none of his business, although I realize that he was just being a friend and looking out for me.

"My Goodness, Rocco's date is really beautiful. Where does he find these women?"

Alex turned to look at the woman seated in front of Rocco. "Yes, she is beautiful. Just Rocco's type." He then turned back to me and said, "But she doesn't hold a candle to the woman that I'm having dinner with tonight."

I couldn't help but laugh a little. It felt so good to get compliments from Alex. It was almost like he truly meant what he was saying.

"So, the doctor is a *smooth operator!*" Alex smiled at my comment and tightened his grip on my hand.

"I mean it, sweetheart. You're beautiful. And you're interesting, and funny, and I can't stop thinking about you when we're apart." The conversation had suddenly turned serious. I tried to free my hand from Alex's grip, but he wouldn't let me.

"Briana, we should leave now. Let's have coffee at your place, OK, unless you really want to stay here longer."

"I'm ready to go too, Alex."

We waved at Rocco as we made our way out of the restaurant. I couldn't help but wonder if Rocco's date would enjoy the night in Rocco's strong arms. Would he hold her all night long and whisper sweet nothings in her ear tonight? Would she wake up to the smell of coffee, bacon, and eggs and eat breakfast in Rocco's gorgeous garden?

As if sensing that I was feeling a little strange, Alex put his arm around my shoulders and kept me to his side as we walked over to his car. He kissed my temple before opening the door to the passenger seat of his car and helping me in.

Once in the car, I turned to Alex as I suddenly realized that we hadn't even spoken about the Foundation. "Alex, didn't you say that you wanted to discuss some fundraising options with me?"

Alex just grinned as he turned to look at me. "I lied, Briana. I just wanted you to come have dinner with me."

I think I knew all along that there was no business to discuss. I didn't mind, though, and I didn't even pretend to feel upset. I just returned Alex's grin with one of my own.

"Alex, please make yourself at home while I make the coffee." It felt a little strange having Alex in my home. He followed me into the kitchen and sat at the table. He must have thought that my home was so plain, bare of any luxuries and cluttered with toys. I certainly couldn't afford the lavish furnishings that he obviously had in his *bachelor's* home.

"It's too bad that your kids aren't here. I would've liked to have seen them. I'm sure that you're a great mom."

"I try to be a good mom. They really are great kids, so I'm pretty lucky."

"You must've looked so beautiful when you were pregnant. You probably breast-fed? Lucky kids!"

Alex had a devilish grin on his face. He even managed to make breast-feeding sound sexy. If he only knew how difficult it had been for me to breast-feed my children. After I had my first child, I breast-fed my son while I had an infection in my nipples. Let me tell you, the pain was worse than child-birth. There was nothing 'beautiful' about that!

I was setting out a tray of cookies when Alex came up behind me. He placed his hands on my hips and his face on the side of my neck. "Alex, don't do that." My voice didn't sound so convincing.

"Why? It feels good, doesn't it?"

"Yes. I mean, no. Please, we had a nice dinner together. Let's not ruin it."

"How could this be ruining it?" He was placing little kisses all along my neck. "This can only add to our evening and make it even better." I could feel that he was grinning.

He turned me so that I was facing him. He pulled me up close and reached back to lightly place his hands on my ass. I could feel myself begin to panic. He then brushed his lips against mine, and I melted in his arms.

"Remember how we made out like a couple of school kids at Rocco's party?" Alex said with a laugh. "Didn't it feel great? I haven't been able to get you out of my mind, Briana. I've been clinging to memories of how you felt in my arms, and how sweet you tasted."

I could feel his breath on my cheek as he spoke. He was so seductive, so sexy, so fuckin' delicious. Oh, to hell with it! It felt so good. Why shouldn't I just enjoy being with Alex? Didn't I deserve a little pleasure in my life?

I put my arms around his neck and kissed the tip of his nose. I'd wanted to do that for so long. We both smiled.

"Briana, you feel so good in my arms." I couldn't help myself any longer. I kissed him on his mouth. I ran my tongue along his lips before slipping it inside of his mouth. I felt his body shudder with delight as I licked him. I tasted his mouth. I slowly licked his tongue, and I could suddenly feel his hardness rub up against my belly. The feel of it made me so hungry for more. I wanted him so badly. I wanted all of him. I craved to take him in my mouth. I wanted to feel his body quiver for me.

Alex lifted me onto the kitchen counter. My legs were now wrapped around him, and my back was leaning against the cupboards. He placed his hand over my breast and gently stroked it over my dress, before reaching through the opening and cupping it. My nipple hardened under his touch. Alex smiled up at me; he placed his mouth on my hard nipple and gently sucked at it.

I reached down and placed my hand on his cock. I was shocked and so pleased to feel that he was so big. My breathing became ragged. I gently bit at his lower lip with my teeth, and I rubbed his cock with my hand. I wanted it inside of me. My need was urgent. I've never wanted anyone as much as I wanted Alex.

With a deep groan, Alex looked at me, a glazed look in his eyes. "Are you sure you want to do this, sweetheart? You're ready, right? Tell me that you want this as much as I do."

At the pleading look in Alex's eyes, I placed my hands on either side of his face and kissed his mouth.

"Tell me, *please*."

"I want you, Alex. I always have." I kissed him, passionately, urgently. "I want you, body and soul. I need you. I've dreamt about you for so long.

You've taken over my dreams, all of my thoughts, my fantasies, and my desires."

Alex sighed, and smiled at me. His look was gentle and kind. "You wouldn't believe the dreams that I've been having about *you* lately!"

"Yeah? Don't tell me about them, show me." I began to kiss him again, all over. I kissed his eyes, nose, and chin. I took his earlobe in between my teeth; I licked it and then sucked on it gently. "I've wanted to do this for so long. I love you so much."

I felt Alex's body stiffen. He lowered his head and moved a little away from me. "Fuck!" he said under his breath.

Yeah, that was exactly what I wanted to do, so what was the matter with Alex?

"Is this your way of getting out of making love with me, Briana?"

I was feeling a little dazed, light-headed. "Alex? What's the matter? I *want* to make love to you."

Alex put his head down, but not before I caught a strange look of bewilderment cross over his face. He ran his hand through his hair and let out a long sigh. "I'm so attracted to you Briana. I enjoy being with you. And I really do care about you. It's because I care about you that I want to be completely honest with you. I never want to mislead you."

"*Please*, Alex." I couldn't believe it, and I just felt like I was being punched in the stomach.

"Briana, don't love me. I don't deserve it.

I already told you that I'm not looking for love. I can't promise you anything right now. Do you understand what I'm saying, sweetheart?"

"I do understand. You want to have sex with me. You don't want to commit to anything, though. You don't want me to love you, because that'll only make you feel guilty."

I got off the counter and placed my dress back into place. My heart hurt, and I couldn't help but feel that this was just *typical* for me.

"You did tell me that you weren't looking for love in your life. But Alex, I accepted that and I just wanted to be with you tonight. So I told you that I loved you. So what? What difference does it make to you, anyways? I wanted to be with you tonight, and you wanted to be with me. What difference does it make if I happen to love you, when I don't expect anything from you?"

It sounded logical, and yet *I* didn't even believe it.

Alex had a desperate look in his eyes. He sounded frustrated as he spoke through grated teeth. "It makes a difference to me if I'm hurting you." He grabbed me by the shoulders and pulled me up close to him. "Don't look at me like that. I can't bear it."

Alex's phone rang, but he seemed to want to ignore it. "Alex, you need to answer that. Just get it already!"

He hesitated for a moment, and then he reached for his phone with a frustrated groan. "Dr.

Ferrante..."

I stepped out of the kitchen and went to sit on the porch. The fresh air felt nice, but I just really needed to get away from Alex. What was I doing? I told him that I was OK with simply having sex with him, even though I loved him, and I didn't expect anything more than sex in return. I was making light of something that was actually very important to me. How could I compromise myself in this way? I wish I could be the type to casually enjoy sex with a man. Of course the problem was that this wasn't going to be sex with just any man. This was going to be sex with the object of all of my fantasies. I loved Alex, and nothing about him could ever be casual for me.

Alex came out on the porch and sat next to me on the swing. He looked tired, stressed out, and a little concerned. "What is it, Alex? Did something happen?"

He took one of my hands in his and just held it in his lap. "There's so much ugliness in this world, Briana. So much pain, you know?" He leaned back and looked out into the darkness.

"That was an old friend of mine that called. Apparently, his son's girlfriend was just told that she has a ten-centimeter tumor on her lungs. He wants me to take her on as a patient. Damn it!

She's eighteen years old."

"Oh my God. Alex, I'm so sorry to hear that."

"I told him to get Emma admitted to my hospital and I'll see her tomorrow. We'll begin with all of the tests and then we'll be able to determine exactly what we're dealing with."

What an awful evening this had turned out to be. A poor young girl was given such horrible news. There really is so much ugliness in the world. I guess we can't lose sight of all of the beauty that there is too. Yes, poor Emma is about to embark on a very scary journey. And yes, thank God that she has Dr. Ferrante, who will do everything possible to make sure that she'll get through it.

"She's lucky that she has you as her doctor." I couldn't even have him as my lover. Was I feeling jealous of a sick young girl? No. Luckily, I haven't reached that level of stupidity yet.

"Would you like that coffee now?" I went to get up, and Alex pulled me back down.

"I think we need to talk about what happened in there, don't you?" There was no desire in his eyes as he looked at me. Only sadness.

"I don't know what's left to say. I won't apologize for how I feel about you, Alex. And you do deserve to be loved. You are strong and courageous enough to devote your life to helping very sick people. You deserve the happiness and love that you allow people to get back when you fight for their lives."

"Oh yeah, and what about you, Briana? Do I

deserve the same kind of happiness that I *inflict* on you?" He gripped my shoulders with his hands, a tortured expression on his face. I wasn't quite sure how to handle this side of Alex. I wanted to comfort him because I could see that he was hurting. But I was hurting too! Was I supposed to comfort him for not loving me in the way that I loved him? This was a little too much for me.

"Maybe you should go home now, Alex. I'm sure you have a very big day ahead of you tomorrow and you need all your strength to be able to tackle it." I wanted him to go. I wanted to be alone so that I could cry my eyes out and just feel sorry for myself. I know that it's weak and just so unproductive to waste time feeling sorry for yourself. But sometimes it just feels so good to have a nice cry. It's very healing.

"I don't want to leave you. I don't want to go. Can't we just sit here for a while longer?" He positioned himself on the swing so that he was lying down on it. I lay on the swing as well, with my back to him and my body cradled up against him. We stayed in that position for a while.

For some reason the universe conspired against me to actually get some sex in my life. How could something so simple for many people be so impossible for me to get? So obviously sex was out of the question for the night, and I wasn't in the mood to console the man responsible for my sexual frustration. I couldn't help but wonder if Rocco was getting his groove on with that woman he was having dinner with earlier that evening. I was feeling a little envious.

Alex left after receiving a second call from his friend. Surprisingly, I slept through the night and woke up the next morning feeling so refreshed. Alex called me by late afternoon.

"Briana, I'm sorry about last night. I actually don't know what to say."

"There's nothing to say, Alex. Don't worry about it." When I first met Alex, when he was treating my mom and we were texting each other, he often told me not to worry about certain inappropriate texts of mine. *How life has changed.*

"How's your young patient doing?"

"It doesn't look too good. We think that she has Hodgkin's lymphoma. Obviously, more tests need to be done before we know for sure. She's going to have a tough road ahead of her."

"There's no doubt in my mind that she is in the best of hands with you as her doctor."

"Briana…" I was waiting for him to finish his sentence, but he didn't say anything.

"What is it, Alex?"

"It was just really nice being with you yesterday. They're paging me now, so I need to go. Will I see you soon?"

"Yeah, sure, Alex. Go ahead, and good luck, OK."

"Thanks, sweetheart."

21

I'm in the Mood for You

So, a few weeks went by and I was able to stay away from Alex. We spoke a couple of times on the phone, but I always kept it very short. I was able to use my family commitments as good excuses for not meeting him for dinner. I think he got the message. I didn't want to be mean, but that last rejection from Alex, well, that was just too much, even for me. Even I have a little pride, sometimes.

I was working from home and enjoying the quiet. The kids were at school, and I had the house all to myself. The shrieking sound of the phone ringing shattered the silence that I had been so enjoying.

"Hello?"

"Hi, Briana. It's Rocco."

"Hi, Rocco. How are you?"

"I'm good. Look, I've got a couple of tickets to the opera tonight and I can't think of anyone else to take. So will you come?"

"Ah, Rocco, I don't know what to say. You're asking me out but it doesn't sound like you're asking me *out*, you know, like on a date."

"That's because it's not a date. *It's Rocco calling, honey, not Alex.* I just know that you like things like the opera, and really, the women that I do date aren't too interested in that kind of thing."

He can be so insulting and so full of shit sometimes! He calls me to ask me out, and then makes me feel so foolish for calling it a date! Like I'm not the kind of girl that someone like him would date! Like I'm not *hot* enough for someone like Rocco!

"OK, take it easy, honey. I could feel you throwing daggers at me through the phone."

"You are just so full of it! Maybe I don't want to be seen with someone like *you,* Rocco."

"Hey, I don't blame you, honey. I wouldn't want to be seen with someone like me either." I could hear the laughter in his voice. "But don't get all sensitive on me, and stop being a baby. Be smart! You love the opera, and I have great seats."

He was right. He was an ass, but he was right

about me loving the opera. I never get to go any-where. Actually, I only just started to go out a little more because of opportunities presented to me by Rocco. Who am I kidding? I don't have any pride and I do love a good opera.

"So, do you have tickets to *Madame Butterfly*?" I actually tried to get tickets to the show, but the tickets were too expensive for me. I couldn't justify spending so much money on a show, not when my kids wanted and needed so much. And besides, I didn't have anyone to go with either.

"That's my girl! Yeah, I have great tickets. Unfortunately, I have a late meeting that I can't get out of, so we can't have dinner before the show. But I'll pick you up at 7 p.m., at your home, and we'll head straight for the show. Are you going to be able to get a sitter for the kids on such short notice?" *Always thoughtful.*

"I'm pretty sure my mom will be able to look after the kids."

"Good. See you later."

It's true that Rocco can be very abrupt. He doesn't mince words. And although his frankness is sometimes a little hurtful, it's also a little wel-comed. I don't have to pretend with him. He knows how to get to me. And I can trust Rocco. He is my friend.

Rocco picked me up at 7 p.m. sharp. He was wearing a blue shirt that made his eyes look a little darker than usual. He looked striking, just oozing with masculinity. He wasn't his usual sarcastic self tonight. He was a little quiet and pensive.

The opera was beautiful. I really do love this type of thing. I'm a real sucker for a beautiful and tragic love story.

I could tell that Rocco enjoyed it too. He really understands and appreciates art. What a strange animal Rocco is. He's so rough, tough, and big, and yet so kind-hearted and gentle. He's so beautiful, and so damaged. *Yeah, tragic.*

At a certain point during the opera, I was feeling so sad and I was holding back my tears. Rocco placed his hand over mine and began to gently caress it with his finger. He kept on watching the show and didn't turn to look at me. I don't know what came over me, but I took his hand and brought it up to my face. I kissed it, pressed it against my cheek, and let my tears fall all over it. Rocco just let me do it. He didn't say a word, nor did he look at me.

When it was over he just grabbed my hand and led me out of the theater and we walked over to his car. Neither of us said anything. We did however, look at each other briefly as we got up from our seats, and simply smiled at each other. But that was it.

"I don't know about you, but I could sure go for some sushi right about now." Rocco was back! He had a great big grin on his face, but I could see that he was still caught up in the whole beauty of it all, as he was rubbing his scar.

"Isn't it a little late to eat? It's past 11 p.m." I

wasn't tired at all and, quite frankly, I wanted to spend more time with Rocco. But I still felt like I should protest for some reason.

"I have a great idea. Just sit back and enjoy the ride." Rocco drove to a sushi restaurant and ordered a whole bunch of takeout food. We then drove to the mountain at Mount Royal Park which was close by, and parked at the lookout. I hadn't done something like this since I was a teenager, and it was great! We ate, we spoke, and we laughed. It was so much fun for me.

"I want to thank you, Rocco, for tonight. For everything. I had a really great time."

"Why, is the evening over? Is this my cue to drive you home now? I thought you were having a *great time*?"

"I am having a great time. But don't all good things have to come to an end? I mean, it's pretty late. Of course, tomorrow is Saturday. It's not a work day."

"Stop rambling on, Briana. Am I making you nervous?"

"Nervous? Not at all. The sushi was good, wasn't it? Are you satisfied now, or are you in the mood for more? Maybe coffee?"

"I'm in the mood for you." At first Rocco just looked at me. Then he reached forward and placed one arm around me, drawing me up to him. We didn't even kiss at first. We just sat together in a very close embrace. I rubbed my lips along his jaw, and my fingers were in his hair. And then he began to kiss me. He kissed my forehead, my eyes, my cheeks, and the tip of my nose, my chin, and finally my mouth. He kissed like he was enjoying it, like he was enjoying me. I felt like I was his dessert, only I was enjoying it too. He held onto me like he owned me, and kissed me like he was taking what was his. It was so intense, and I felt like I was shaking with excitement. I have to admit that it felt good to have a man take charge over me in the way that Rocco did, but I wanted to see how he would react if I tried to take a little bit of control over for myself. I slipped my tongue in his mouth and began to lick him, slowly and thoroughly. I was so into it. But then I felt him shudder. I realized that he was laughing.

"What the fuck, Rocco!" I tried to push him away, but he kept hold of me.

"I'm sorry, sweetheart. I'm not laughing at you; it's just that I can't believe that a little slip of a woman could have this effect on me. And where did you learn to kiss like that?"

"Well, don't think that you'll ever get any more of that from me. It was simply a temporary lapse of sanity on my part."

"Temporary lapse of sanity! Don't talk that way about what happened between us. It was hot and sexy, and you know it. Come on, honey, I want some more." Rocco held the back of my head and began kissing me again, all over my face.

It wasn't hard to give in, and I quickly began returning his hungry kisses with a wild, passionate hunger of my own. We kissed for such a long time. It was passionate, wild, and hungry.

It was so hard to do, but I finally managed to pull my tongue out of his mouth and place it back into mine. "I need to get back. My mom is at my house with the kids, and I just know that she's probably not going to get to sleep until I'm home."

"Sure, Briana." Rocco wiped his mouth with his thumb and turned the car on. "I'll take you home now."

We drove to my home in silence. I think we both weren't quite sure how to handle what had just happened. I don't think either of us was surprised, though. I considered Rocco a good friend, but I wasn't immune to his virile good looks. For a while now I had felt a chemistry brewing between us, and I guess Rocco felt it too. I didn't have the guts to ask him how he felt, though. I would play it by ear.

I was a little disappointed when we got to my home. I didn't want to leave him. Rocco was the first to speak. "Briana, I have a dinner party to go to on Sunday night. A bunch of my clients will be there, along with some important benefactors from the Foundation." He had a strange look on his face and was rubbing his scar. "I want you to come with me. Be ready for 6:30 p.m."

"Rocco, you can't just treat me like that! If you want me to come with you, ask me nicely. Like the suave gentleman that I know you are. Why are you like this only with me? I see you with other women, and you're so nice with them. But with me, it's like you are resentful somehow."

"Maybe I am a little resentful."

"Why? Aren't we supposed to be friends? I think of you as a great person and I really value your friendship. I don't even *resent* you for bullying your way into my life." I laughed a little, but I really wasn't amused.

"*Friends? Really?* Do you kiss all of your friends like that, Briana? I hope not!" He had the audacity to have a look of disgust on his face.

"OK, let's stop this right now. Do you want me to come with you to your dinner party, Rocco?"

"Yes."

"OK then, I'd love to come with you."

"Briana, Alex will be there." Rocco turned and looked at me intently as if he was trying to read my expression.

"That's fine, Rocco. Alex and I are OK."

"Do you love him?"

He caught me off guard with that one. I hesitated and then opted for the truth. "Yes."

Rocco looked away, a strange look on his face. It was a look of neither anger nor disappointment. Was he a little upset that I loved Alex? And then he looked at me again. "Are you *in love* with him?"

"I think so. Alex and I are not together, but we are on good terms. I guess you can say that we're friends."

"He's your *friend*, Briana? The same *kind* of friend that you have in me?"

I knew what Rocco wanted to hear. "No, Rocco, nobody could be like you." It felt a little intense, so I wanted to lighten the mood. I reached over and tapped his hand with mine. "You are my buddy."

Rocco looked at me and actually looked a little annoyed. "OK, Briana. Go inside now and I'll see you on Sunday."

I tried to reach over to kiss him goodnight, but he wasn't having any of that. He just moved away and turned his head the other way. "Goodnight, Rocco, and thank you for tonight."

I know that Rocco was annoyed with me. He never did like the idea of Alex and me being together. He believed that Alex was going to hurt me. Well, he doesn't have to worry about that. As long as I love him, Alex won't touch me with a ten-foot pole.

22

Praise the Lord Almighty!

That night was a strange one for me. I couldn't sleep. I had a very uneasy feeling, and it scared me a little because I often get these premonitions. The morning after, bright and early, I learned that I had every reason to feel scared.

Alex called me bright and early. He was working at the hospital. "Good morning, Briana. How are you?"

"Hi, Alex. I'm good, thanks. How are you? You're at work early today."

"Briana, Rocco was in a car accident last night. He was admitted to my hospital. He has suffered a concussion, but I think that he's going to be OK. I thought you would want to know."

"Oh my God. Alex, is he really OK? Please be honest with me."

"Of course I'm being honest with you. He'll be fine. He's actually pretty lucky. He was hit head-on by a drunk driver. It could've been a lot worse. He'll probably be released later on today."

"I'll be there as soon as possible. Thanks for calling me."

I felt so bad for Rocco. If we had only stayed together a little while longer, well, maybe this wouldn't have happened to him. I got dressed and made my way to the hospital as quickly as I could.

Rocco was asleep in bed when I got to the hospital. I sat by his side and just waited until he woke up. Being there, in that little room, took me back to when my mom was in the hospital. She was so sick and in so much pain. It was such a difficult time for us, but thank God *and Alex*, we got through it and I still have my mom in my life today. And some things don't change, because when I was thinking about Alex, well, he walked right in the room, just like when I used to sit by my mom's hospital bed.

"Hi, Briana. Oh, Rocco is still sleeping. Luckily he'll be just fine." Alex came in closer and hugged me close to him. "It's so nice of you to come so quickly. How are you feeling today?"

"I'm good, Alex. I'm glad that Rocco is going to

be fine. You must be exhausted, though. Have you been here all night?"

"Yes, I have. I didn't want to leave while Rocco was still here. But I'm fine. I'll go home soon."

"Hey there, come a little closer so that I can hear what you guys are saying." Rocco was awake.

"Hi, Rocco." I leaned over and gave Rocco a few kisses on his forehead. "How are you feeling? You scared the hell out of me!"

Rocco smiled at me and slowly answered my question. "I'm fine, maybe just a little tired. Hey, Alex, when can I leave this place?"

"Glad to see that you're all better, Rocco. I'll go find out about your release papers, and then you'll be able to go. Just take it easy for the next few days, OK, Roc?"

"Alex, thank you," Rocco called out as Alex was about to leave the room.

"Don't mention it, buddy. I'm just glad that you're OK." Alex looked at me with those eyes that I had fallen in love with a while ago now, and he flashed that smile that could bring me to my knees. And then he was gone.

I turned to Rocco and grabbed his hand. "I'm so happy that you're OK. If we hadn't gone out last night, this wouldn't have happened to you."

"Don't be ridiculous, Briana. Accidents happen. And I'm fine."

"Did you call your family? Want me to call them for you?"

"No, Briana, I don't want them to worry for

nothing. I didn't want Alex to call you either. And besides, I'll be leaving here shortly. I think I'll get up now and get my things together."

"I'll drive you home, Rocco."

Rocco shook his head. "I'll take a cab."

"No, Rocco. I'm coming home with you, and that's final. You can rest, and I'll be there in case you need something from me. I won't leave you alone tonight. Just be quiet and accept it. You took care of me when I needed it, remember, and so let me do the same for you now."

We got to Rocco's home by early afternoon. I told him to get into bed and to try to get some sleep. I was so pleased to see that his fridge and pantry were full of groceries. His housekeeper does such a good job running his home. I had everything I needed to prepare some chicken soup. Somehow, chicken soup always seems to be the perfect answer to cure whatever ails you.

By early evening, Rocco was up and had even showered. "How are you feeling, Rocco?"

"I feel good, Briana, really. It's not necessary for you to be doing this."

"Would you like me to leave, Rocco? Because I want to be here, but if my presence bothers you…"

"No, don't take it like that. I just don't want to take you away from your kids."

"*Stop it*. I'm here, and I cooked, so let's eat, OK?"

We ate together in the kitchen. He has such a beautiful kitchen. It was a pleasure to set the table, using the beautiful plates, glassware, and cutlery. After supper we watched a movie together in the family room. I couldn't help feeling so sad for Rocco. His beautiful home should be filled with a big family, his wife, and children. Rocco would've been a great dad.

"Rocco, get in bed now. I think you need to get to bed early." I noticed that he winced a little as he made his way up the stairs to his room.

"What is it, Rocco? Are you hurt? Do you feel pain?"

"I just hurt my leg a little. It's a little stiff, that's all."

I followed Rocco into his room. He was a little surprised to see me there. I went into his bathroom and found some body cream.

"OK, Rocco. Just lie down and relax. I will rub your legs with this cream."

"What? Ah no, honey. Thank you, but that's really not necessary."

I ignored his protests. Maybe he was a little embarrassed to let someone do things for him. He was so used to being the caregiver. I got on my knees on the foot of the bed. He was wearing a white T-shirt and black cotton sports shorts. I squirted some cream in my hands and began rubbing his feet. Rocco and I couldn't help ourselves from grinning at each other.

"Is this OK, Rocco? Am I hurting you?"

"No, it's fine."

"Just close your eyes then, and let yourself

fall asleep."

I continued to rub his feet and calves. I was moving my way up his legs. Boy, did Rocco ever have a good body. He was so hard! His legs were long, lean, and muscular. Truthfully, I was enjoying massaging his body. I was looking forward to the prospect of massaging his back and chest. *Shameful!*

"Rocco?" He opened his eyes and looked up at me.

"How are your legs feeling? A little better? Still stiff?"

Rocco smiled a little and ran his hands through his hair. "All better, thanks. No stiffness, at least not in my legs!"

"Take off your shirt, and I'll do your back." Rocco obliged without uttering any protests this time. He turned around and lay on his belly.

He is so broad, so the best way to do him was to sit on his bum, with my legs spread wide apart. I squirted cream on his back and began to rub the muscled hardness of his arms, shoulders, and back. What a fine specimen indeed!

"Your jeans are a little rough against my skin, Briana. Could you take them off, please?"

"Are you serious?"

"Hey, it's nothing that I haven't already seen." He was referring to that night that we spent together in this very same bed.

I was being a little hypocritical, as I was surely enjoying looking at his body. And my jeans were as uncomfortable to have on as they were obviously rough on his skin. So I decided to take them off.

"OK, but don't turn around."

I got right back on him and continued to massage his strong, beautiful body. Rocco's even breathing told me that he was fast asleep. I didn't want to stop touching him, though. How desperate! His hair was tousled, and I just really wanted to run my fingers through it. What harm could running my fingers through his hair really do? I leaned forward so that I was lying right over his back and I touched the hair at his neck with my hand. Before I knew it, I brought my face close to the back of his neck. I inhaled deeply, wanting to smell his masculine scent. I gently placed my lips on his neck and kissed him.

At that point Rocco turned over so quickly that I hardly knew what was happening, and he grabbed hold of me in his arms. He looked at me intently right in the eyes, and he didn't say anything at all. After a few moments, he began to kiss me. His kisses were gentle. Loving rather than hungry. But the hardness rubbing up against me was anything but gentle. I could feel that he wanted me, urgently, and yet all I could get from him was some gentle kissing. Maybe he wasn't well, and I was pushing him too far.

I looked up and moved a little away from him. Rocco was just quietly looking at me, expressionless. "Are you OK, Rocco? Are you feeling sick?" I placed my hand on his forehead to feel if he was warm, but he felt fine.

"Rocco?"

"Do you know what you're doing, Briana? Because when you touch me and kiss me like that, well, let's just say that there's only so much that I can do to stay in control."

"Maybe I want you to lose control, Rocco, because when I look at you there's only so much that I can do to stay in control too."

He just kept looking at me. I could see that he was conflicted. Should he? Shouldn't he? *I* know that *I* wanted him. I wanted to be in his arms. I wanted to kiss him, to taste him, and to feel his manhood in my hands, my mouth, and inside of me.

I sure loved him, although I don't know if I was *in love* with him. Could taking our relationship to the next level ruin a relationship that had come to mean very much to me? I hope not, but I was willing to risk it. Rocco was probably thinking the same thing that I was. Maybe he just wasn't attracted to me and didn't want to hurt my feelings. But sometimes we need to take risks.

I got on my knees just next to Rocco, on the bed, and I began to unbutton my shirt. I took off my shirt and waited for him to make a move. I was beginning to panic when Rocco finally said something.

"Are you sure about this, Briana?"

I just nodded in agreement. "Rocco, *I'm in the*

mood for you."

That did it. He reached out for me and pulled me into his arms. He sat me on top of him, and kissed me. He licked my lips with his sexy tongue before slipping it in my mouth. He then expertly took my bra off and began to kiss my tits. He squeezed them at first and just looked at them with a look of pure pleasure on his face. He then used that sexy tongue of his to lick my nipples. He slipped one in his mouth and sucked a little. He did the same to my other nipple but sucked a little harder this time. It was so good, and I was in ecstasy.

But I wanted to feel his hardness and I began to wiggle my body over him to try to entice him to give it to me. We shifted positions, and I was now lying on the bed next to him. He kissed me briefly before he pulled my panties off, and he also quickly removed his clothing.

Good golly! Rocco was naked; he was huge and so sexy! I was a little shocked by my need. I was just so excited over him. I tried to reach for Rocco, but he beat me to it. He grabbed me close to him and he lifted my leg up so that he could more easily slide his big cock right inside of me. He was penetrating me, but I could feel that he was resisting a little. He was huge, but so good and I wanted so much more of him. I tried to push him closer to me by holding on to his taut, gorgeous ass. I could feel my nails digging into him.

"Am I hurting you, baby? Can you handle me?"

"Oh yes, I can handle you! It's so good. You're so good, Rocco. *You're so delicious*."

This tipped him over the edge. He let out a groan, penetrated me deeply, and cried my name out in pleasure.

"Oh yes, Rocco. You do me so good. Come for me, baby! Come inside of me. I want you all over me!"

Praise the Lord Almighty! I transcended into heaven. I think I literally saw stars when I came and I'm pretty sure that I heard gospel music. I knew Rocco would be a good, strong lover. He really didn't disappoint.

When it was over and we finally caught our breaths, I was lying in bed in Rocco's arms. He was rubbing my arm and then he kissed my forehead.

"Any regrets, Briana?"

"None. And you?"

"No."

"You're a sex machine, Rocco! I think you might be great at just about everything and anything that you do!"

We both laughed, and Rocco spanked my bum a little as he faked shock at my words.

"Stay in bed, Rocco, and I'll go get you a snack. Then you should get some sleep." I kissed Rocco on the mouth, pulled my T-shirt on, and headed down to the kitchen to prepare that snack.

Wow! No turning back now. But no, no regrets at all. I felt great and so satisfied. I actually couldn't wait to be with him again. I never did get a chance to taste all of him, and I was really looking forward to it. I probably should have felt ashamed at being so wanton. But I just felt good instead.

So I washed and cut up some fruit and placed it on a tray along with some crackers and cheese. Rocco was in the washroom when I got into bed. He was still completely naked when he came back to bed, and I couldn't help but hungrily stare at his sexy, virile naked body as he walked across the room and made his way back to bed.

Rocco noticed me staring at him as he walked over to me. He grinned, bent his head a little, and began to rub his scar. If I didn't know him any better I would say that he was feeling a little embarrassed. But embarrassed about what? Was he embarrassed about what had happened between us, or was it that he caught me enjoying his nakedness? He was definitely thinking about something, though, because he was rubbing his scar. Yeah, I would definitely kiss his scar later on and take all of his worries away.

"Come, *lover*." I patted the bed just next to me with my hand. "Come have some fruit with me." I was feeling happy, and I couldn't stop myself from showing it. We ate in bed and watched some sitcom on TV. It was nice, and I didn't want it to end.

"How are you feeling, Rocco? Does your head hurt?"

"I'm feeling pretty good right now. You might have a little to do with that. You sure know how to take care of a patient." He grinned, pulled the covers over himself, and snuggled up closer to me. "But I am a little tired, so I think that I'm going to sleep now."

"Rocco?"

"Yeah?"

"Can I stay with you in your bed tonight?" Oddly enough, I didn't even feel embarrassed asking him a question that I would normally consider to be incredibly desperate.

Rocco looked at me with such tenderness on his face. He reached out and pulled me into his arms. He kissed me gently on the mouth. "Go to sleep now."

I did sleep, deeply. I slept better than I had in a very long time. It felt so good to be in Rocco's arms. He made me feel safe.

Was I dreaming? I could still feel Rocco's love-making, and my body was responding. It was 3:30 a.m., and I was being awakened by Rocco's gentle caressing kisses all over my body. I was a little confused at first, but I could see Rocco's grinning face in the darkness. I quickly realized that I was in his bed and it was the middle of the night.

Rocco pulled me on top of his body, and his hands were all over me. He was grabbing my ass and rubbing me up against his body. He began sucking on my nipples and gently running his finger down the crack of my ass. He kept his finger at the very bottom of my quivering vagina and stroked me with a circular motion.

I thought that I was going to pass out. I held onto Rocco and bit him on his shoulder.

"You little tiger!" Rocco was being playful, but I wasn't in the mood for kidding around.

"I think I'm going to keep biting you until you give me what I want!"

"What do you want, baby? Tell me."

"I want your big cock inside of me and I want you to fuck me!"

Rocco was taken aback by my dirty talk, but after a few seconds he just laughed and turned me over. I was lying on my back on the bed, and he was slightly over me. He spread my legs open and inserted first one, then two fingers inside of me.

"You're so wet." Rocco kissed me, and his sexy tongue was inside of my mouth. His voice was husky. "Tell me you want me."

"You know I do."

"Still, I like hearing it."

"I want you, Rocco. You're driving me crazy! You're so hot!" I kissed him. "And strong." I kissed him again. "And sexy." I couldn't stop the kisses. "And you're a great lover. You know how to fuck me so good. You have a fucking hot body, and your cock is so big!"

Rocco was inside of me before I had time to finish verbalizing how much I wanted him. We both came at the same time. We stayed in each other's arms for a while. It was great.

When I noticed that Rocco was dozing off, I snuggled up closer to him and kissed his beautiful scar. I kissed my handsome, strong, loyal, and brilliant Rocco. We slept the rest of the night locked in each other's arms.

It was nearly 10 a.m. when the phone's ringing woke us. Rocco and I both looked at each other briefly before realizing that it was the phone. Then Rocco smiled at me and reached for the phone. It was obvious that he was feeling just as strange as I was about what had happened between us. What we shared was awesome, but was Rocco still my best friend, or was he now my lover? I'm sure that he was thinking the same thing as me.

Rocco was talking to Alex on the phone. "No, Alex, you didn't wake me. I'm doing fine. I got a lot of rest and I actually feel very refreshed. Those pills that you prescribed must be amazing, because I haven't felt this good in a long time." Rocco looked at me and winked, grinning. "No, you don't have to come by, but thanks for offering. Besides, Briana has been with me and she's been an excellent caregiver. Oh yeah, she hasn't left my side. Alright, Alex. Thanks for calling." He then suddenly looked very serious and added, "And thanks for everything, Alex. Thanks for being a good friend."

"Don't look at me like that, Briana. I don't want it to get weird between us."

"I'm not looking at you in any weird way. Was that Alex calling to see how you're doing?"

"Yeah, it was Alex. Feeling guilty about cheating on the love of your life, Briana? Are you sorry that you spent the night with me?" Rocco's voice was rough and angry, but the look on his face was anything but angry. Actually, he almost looked a little tortured. It made me feel so bad. The only thing that I was sorry about was being responsible for causing Rocco some pain.

Rocco was sitting up in bed. I reached forward and put my arms around his neck. I kissed his scar and snuggled up closer into his arms. "How could I be sorry about spending the night with you? Not only are you an amazing lover"—I could feel him softening up— "but it just feels so right with you. I love being in your arms, Rocco."

"So you're not denying that he's the love of your life?"

"OK, Rocco, now you sound like a teenager! What's all this about *the love of your life*? You already know that I love Alex. I always have. I don't know why I feel this way about him, but he doesn't feel the same way about me. And there's nothing but friendship between us."

"We're friends too, Briana."

"Yes, we are. But we're special friends."

"Are you saying that we're friends with benefits? I don't think I like the sound of that and I think that it's a little disgusting coming from you."

"I did not mean that! You're my best friend, Rocco, and I love you. I haven't been intimate with Alex. I don't go around sleeping with my friends or anyone else for that matter. It's different with you, Rocco. And I don't know what to make of *this* either. Please don't question my morals, Rocco, and don't doubt my friendship to you. I didn't plan this. And I can't change some things in my life, or how I feel about certain people. I won't ever judge you, Rocco. Please show me the same consideration. Don't forget that I've seen the kinds of women that you date. I'm nothing like them, but I won't let my insecurities get in the way of our friendship."

"You never have to feel insecure." Rocco hugged me and kissed me on the forehead. "You're perfect just the way that you are. Sure, you're so clumsy and goofy sometimes"—he squeezed my arm and laughed a little— "but perfect nonetheless."

We had a good talk, but somehow it just seemed a little strange to be in bed with Rocco in broad daylight. Nighttime was different. Maybe it was just easier to give in to wanton urges in the darkness, but the daylight seems to highlight everything and just sober you into reality.

"I'll go prepare breakfast for you, Rocco."

"Let's do it together. I'm all better now, so you don't have to worry anymore."

I quickly got dressed, brushed my teeth, and made my way downstairs to meet Rocco. When I got there, I noticed Rocco standing in front of his late wife's portrait in the living room. He was just looking at her, his shoulders somehow slumped. He had a look of defeat and pain on his face. It hurt me to see him like that. I didn't want him to feel sad, and honestly I was also beginning to feel something that closely resembled jealousy. Could I be jealous of a dead woman? I guess so. I never had anyone love me intensely. I know that it's so stupid of me, but I couldn't help thinking that when Rocco's time would come and he would die, well, he'd cross over right into Angela's loving arms. Who would come for me when my time came? Nobody, that's who. I quietly made my way into the kitchen.

We made breakfast and ate together, mostly in silence. "Briana, will you still accompany me to the dinner party tonight?"

"I will, but are you sure that you still want to go?"

"Sure, I'm fine now. It's an important dinner. There will be too many important clients, so I can't brush it off. And besides, my *nurse* will be there with me, so I'll be fine. But can you stay away from your kids again tonight? It's too much to ask of you, so maybe you shouldn't come with me."

"I spoke to them just before breakfast, and they are fine. They're having a great time. My mom took them to my sister's house. They're having fun with my niece and nephew. So it's not a problem for me to come with you tonight. I'll just go home and change my clothes, then I'll be back to pick you up."

"No, I'll pick you up."

"Will you stop it! You are not allowed to drive for a few days, and you know it. I'll be your nurse, and your chauffeur."

23

You Rock My World

S hortly after breakfast I went to spend some time with my kids. I was feeling happy, sad, confused, and anxious. I didn't know how I should be feeling. My kids always help me feel better when something is wrong. Marco and Elisa make me feel relaxed and they give me strength to face whatever is bothering me. I was feeling a little guilty about having spent the night away from them. However, they had a nice evening planned with my mom, who was going to take them to the movies, so I felt a little better about leaving them for another evening.

It was just past 6:30 p.m., and Rocco was getting into my car. We were at the dinner party twenty minutes later. Rocco looked great, as usual. Dark skin and hair, light eyes, tall, and built. I guess I looked OK too. I try to stick to black clothing when I don't really know what to wear, so I just wore a tight-fitting little black dress. The neckline was décolleté, and it really made my boobs look pretty nice, actually.

Rocco and I were having a drink in the parlor when we both noticed Alex in the adjoining room speaking with a group of people. "Oh look, Rocco. There's Alex. I guess he didn't notice that we're here, otherwise he would've come over."

Rocco looked at me with his eyebrow raised. "Oh, I'm pretty sure he noticed that we're here, Briana. I mean, really, who wouldn't notice you dressed like that! The girls are practically spilling out of your dress!"

Uhhhhh! How dare he? "The girls look just fine! They are not spilling out. I think that my cleavage is tasteful. You make it sound like I look indecent! And just look at all of the other women in this place. Now *that's* spilling out!" I motioned toward a few women standing close by who really had their girls spilling out!

I could've continued to yell, quietly, at Rocco, but we noticed Alex making his way toward us. "Good evening." Alex smiled and greeted both Rocco and me. "Rocco, how are you feeling? I'm surprised that you made it tonight."

"I'm doing real good, Alex. Thanks. I needed to come out tonight. I spent all day yesterday and today cooped up at home and bored out of my mind! I couldn't spend another minute locked up at home. I can't do *bed rest*, you know. It's just not me."

How dare he? *Bored out of his mind?* What an asshole! Was he trying to hurt me?

"Yeah, I do know what you mean. But at least you had Briana here to help you out a little." Alex looked at me tenderly. I guess he thought of me as a "Florence Nightingale" type. Wonder how he would feel if he learned that I acted like an unchaste and wanton woman while I should've been caring for Rocco.

"By the way, Briana, you look stunning." Alex leaned in closer to me and touched my cheek with his finger.

I felt butterflies in my belly. "You look pretty good yourself, Alex." I could feel Rocco fuming. Good! *Bored out of his mind!*

"And, well, you know what Rocco is like. Right, Alex? So you can imagine that I needed to get out just as much as he did. Maybe more!"

Alex laughed. "Come on, guys." Alex took my hand and led me away. "There's a delicious spread of food laid out in the next room. Let's eat." Rocco followed behind, still fuming. I made eye contact with Rocco and could definitely see that he was angry. Strangely enough, he also had a questioning look in his eyes. He looked like he was trying to read what I was feeling. I couldn't help but raise my upper lip a little, as if to snarl at him. I was feeling angry too.

Throughout the evening, both Rocco and Alex worked the room and schmoozed the right people in the hopes of getting funding for the Foundation. Both were shameless flirts who stood next to women in "way too close for comfort" positions.

Alex and I were alone together for a few minutes at a certain point in the evening. "Briana, you've been avoiding me. You don't answer my calls or my texts. I've been dying to see you and to really talk things out with you."

"Alex, you know where I live and where I work. It couldn't have been too hard to find me if you really wanted to see me."

Alex shook his head in disagreement and took my hand. "No, that's not fair, Briana. I felt terrible about how we ended things the last time that we went out. When you weren't answering my texts, well, I knew that you didn't want to speak to me, and I thought that I should give you some space. I couldn't believe that I hurt you, especially since I care so much about you. Please, Briana..."

"You look like you're having a very intense conversation. Is everything OK?" Rocco loomed over us like a dark storm cloud. One look at Rocco, and I just knew. *Oh yeah, that storm is a comin' and it's gonna be a bad one!"*

Alex looked annoyed as hell at the intrusion. "Everything is good, Rocco, although *you are* interrupting."

"Well, maybe this isn't the place for scenes."

Rocco spoke slowly and with meaning.

Alex faced him. He seemed like he was going to respond quickly but then thought better of it. "You know, I think that you're right. This isn't the place." Alex turned to me with a pleading look in his eyes.

"Briana, will you please have dinner with me sometime this week? Any night, you pick."

Rocco was still standing close by and listening to our conversation. I hesitated at first and then simply agreed. "Sure, Alex. Let me call you tomorrow and we'll decide on a night, OK?"

A short while later, it was time to leave the party. I drove to Rocco's home, and we pretty much drove all the way in silence. "Come in, Briana," Rocco called out as he removed his tall body from my car.

"It's late, Rocco, so I think that I'll just go on home now."

"Do you really think that I'm going to let you drive home by yourself at this late hour? Get in the house, Briana. I'll call you a cab, and you can pick up your car tomorrow."

I knew that arguing with Rocco was useless, especially since he was in such a bad mood.

Once inside, Rocco went to fix himself a drink and handed me a Diet Coke. "I know that you can't handle your liquor."

"What is the matter with you? Why are you so angry? I'm the one that should be angry with you, Rocco. And I am, by the way. You were *bored out of your mind?*"

"What was I supposed to say, that you *fucked* me back to good health?"

We were silent for what seemed like an eternity. "Didn't you enjoy being with me, Rocco? Am I really that boring?"

I had to look away because I could feel the threat of stinging tears in my eyes. "I guess I'm too boring in comparison to the beautiful, experienced women that you're used to and like."

Rocco reached forward and placed his finger on the bottom of my chin. He turned my face and looked into my eyes. "You are not boring. Don't you see that you rock my world?" Now it was Rocco's turn to look away.

I rock *his* world? "Rocco, I've seen the kind of women that you sleep with. They are so beautiful and sexy. I guess I do understand if you find me unsatisfactory."

"You're so stupid, you know that?" Rocco took me in his arms. "You were looking at Alex with hearts shooting out of your eyes! And you looked at him in that way even after the lovemaking that we shared." Rocco looked at me with disbelief on his face.

"I wasn't bored at all, Briana. Being with you was unbelievable. I was just a little surprised that it wasn't enough to make you forget about Alex."

"It was good, wasn't it, between *us*, I mean?"

Rocco ignored my question. "I don't think that he's right for you, Briana."

I could feel Rocco's cock rub up against me. *God!* He was so big! I instinctively rubbed my body against his hardness. I was so wet, and I really wanted him again.

"You belong with me." He leaned over, placed one arm under my knees, and picked me up in his arms. We looked into each other's eyes the whole way as he carried me to his room. It was like a scene out of a *telenovela*. If I hadn't been so turned on, I would've laughed my brains out.

"You know, you didn't have to carry me. I would've willingly run over here, but thanks for the ride."

"*Fuck!* You're so sexy!" He placed me on the bed and began to undress me.

I pulled away from him as he undid my bra. "You do *like* me, right, Rocco? Don't I turn you on, a little?"

Rocco just smiled but didn't say a word. He placed his mouth on my breast and kissed me.

"Rocco?"

"Yes, I like you."

"Rocco?"

"Are you fishing for compliments, Briana?"

He hurt my feelings! Yes, I was fishing for compliments. I tried to get off the bed, but Rocco just pulled me back down.

"Let me go! I don't want to be with you!"

"No, I won't let you go, and you do want to be with me."

"Why do you want me here if you don't even

find me attractive?"

"Did you fall on your head or something? *Do I find you attractive*? You gotta be kidding me!"

His grasp on my wrists softened. "You don't know what you do to me. I want you so badly, Briana." His voice was very low and husky. "You came into my life and somehow, before I knew it, I was obsessing about your beautiful little body, your round little ass, and your delicious tits." He pulled me up and sat me on top of him. My legs were wrapped around his waist.

I smiled at him, and it felt so good to hear him say those things to me. I was so starved for attention. I just wanted to feel attractive. Was that so bad?

"Now why was it so hard for you to say that?" I kissed his face, his nose, his forehead, and his beautiful scar. "I find it so easy to tell you how good-looking you are. You're so handsome, Rocco, and your body is just awesome. I love looking at it, and I really enjoy touching you." I reached back and slid my hands down his back. I began to give him endless kisses on his neck, his shoulders, his ears, and his face. Rocco was squeezing my ass and gently rocking it back and forth against his massive manhood.

Rocco dropped his head back and closed his eyes. He was leaving it up to me. He always takes such good care of me, so the least that I could do was return the favor.

I rubbed my breasts against his hard chest.

I began to kiss and lick him on his chest, and I slowly worked my way down. I wanted to taste all of him. He was so virile.

He jerked a little when I first took him in my mouth. "Just relax, Rocco. Lie back and let me love you, OK."

I began by slowly licking my way up and down his big, long cock. He tasted good and smelled nice.

I couldn't believe myself, as I'd never really liked giving a blow job before. It grossed me out. But here I was, licking away as if I was trying to keep my ice-cream cone from melting down my hand. I was definitely a different person nowadays. Since I'd met Alex, just hearing the words "big cock" could get me so excited. But I have to say, it only works if I think of Alex. And, well, now it works with Rocco too.

I also gently licked his testicles, and he seemed to really like that. What the fuck was I doing? I didn't know, and I didn't care. I just let my instincts take over for me. Hey, Rocco seemed to be enjoying it, so I couldn't have been so far off.

I finally took him in my mouth and began to suck, gently at first, and then with more urgency. Rocco let me go at my own pace, but as his need became more urgent, he began to slowly insert himself deeper and deeper into my mouth.

Thanks to the column that I write, I know that not having a quick gag reflex is supposedly a sexy thing. Well, let me tell you, I was not blessed with that. I absolutely do have a quick gag reflex!

Not too sexy. But, seriously, you would have to be totally abnormal not to gag, because Rocco was so fuckin' huge! Still, I tried my best not to gag too much, as I really did enjoy it and I wanted him to enjoy it too. He finally reached down and pulled me up to him.

"You have to stop now, because I can't handle anymore. I want to continue making love to every inch of your beautiful body."

Our kisses seemed wilder now, out of control. We were all over each other. He inserted his finger inside of me, and that's when I objected.

"Oh no, that's not enough for me right now. I want that big, hot cock of yours inside of me."

Rocco laughed a little and continued to torment me with his finger. "I'm serious. I want you inside of me, now."

I pushed him back on the bed and sat on top of him. He was inside of me, and I was in heaven. I came so fast. So did Rocco.

I felt so satisfied. It was such a good feeling. I was in Rocco's arms, safe and happy. I snuggled up really close to him and nuzzled my nose against his neck. I was gently kissing him there. "Rocco?"

He turned to face me and kissed my forehead. "What is it, honey?"

"You're so good to me, but sometimes you can be a little mean. It just seems like you're angry with me and you want to intentionally hurt my feelings. You don't have to be jealous about Alex, you know. What you and I have is very special to me."

"I'm not jealous, Briana. I just don't think that Alex is right for you. And I don't want to be mean to you. I'm sorry about that. You know me, Bri, and I come with a lot of baggage."

"So, who would be right for me, Rocco?"

"You need someone who's going to be good to you. Someone who's going to appreciate how special you are, and who will be able to take care of you in the way that you deserve. Someone who's going to love your kids too."

"Sounds like you're describing Alex to me! He's smart, kind, a real caregiver, you know? He's a doctor after all!"

"OK, that's enough, Briana." Rocco looked a little irritated. "How can you be thinking about him after what we've just shared?"

I could see that Rocco was hurt, and that was the last thing I wanted. I put both of my hands on the sides of his face and turned him toward me. I kissed him long, but gently, on his mouth. "I'm not thinking about him. I'm thinking about how you can be so loving with me, most of the time, and then let your stupid jealousy over my relationship with Alex make you get a little mean with me. Don't be like that, Rocco. It's not fair."

"*Fair*? Are you kidding…" I shut him up by planting a big wet kiss on his mouth.

"*How am I supposed to feel, Rocco*? You're still in love with your wife. She's the only woman that you've ever loved, and you haven't let yourself get really close to anyone else since. You have a shrine to her in your office and all over your house. Talk about intimidating." Rocco tensed up when I mentioned his wife.

Rocco was very silent. He looked away from me. Obviously the very mention of his late wife was enough to make him sad.

"I'm sorry, Rocco..."

"She's dead, Briana. You can't feel *intimidated* by a dead woman."

"I can't compete with a memory, or a ghost."

"There's no competition. She's dead and gone, and I don't want to speak of this again."

I regretted speaking to Rocco about his wife and about Alex. We had such a nice intimate time together, and I ruined it. I also understood in that moment that I could never be *the one* in this relationship. I would never be on the top of his "love priority list." He'd already married the love of his life. So what if she was dead! That spot at the top of his list was already taken. I never had that with anyone. I certainly didn't have it with my husband, and I lived that way for years. It didn't feel good, and I would never go back to that. So what could I do? I would not allow myself to fall in love with anyone who didn't have that spot at the top of the list vacant! So, Rocco was an emotional cripple because he was still in love with his dead wife. OK. He was also strong and loyal, a great friend, and an incredible lover. I realized I should just be grateful for what we did have and not obsess over what we didn't or could never have.

It was getting really late, and I needed to get back home. I needed to get back to my life, my real life, my priorities. I made to get up, and Rocco grabbed my hand.

"Where are you going?" His eyes were narrowed and he looked like he didn't want me to leave.

"I need to get back home, Rocco."

Rocco pulled me back onto the bed, next to him. He brought my hand up to his mouth and kissed it. "I did it, didn't I? I hurt you. It's the last thing I wanted."

"I know that, Rocco. I don't want to hurt you either. Don't worry, really, we're OK. OK?"

"Stay with me tonight?" The vulnerable look on Rocco's face tore at my heart. I knew how hard it was for him to open himself up to me, or to anyone.

"I need to get back to my kids, Rocco."

"Of course you do. I'm sorry. I don't know what I was thinking."

I put my arms around him and kissed him on his lips. "I would love to stay with you tonight. I don't want to go. I need to go."

"I'm driving you home."

"NO. You're still taking medication, and you can't drive while taking it. Besides, I have my car, and I will be just fine." Rocco didn't look convinced, so I had to be firmer. "I am driving myself home." I hugged him and kissed him again. "I'll call you when I get home. OK, my love?"

He softened up at my words of endearment

and hugged me tight. We soon began kissing again, and as tempted as I was to grab hold of his manhood, which was getting bigger by the second, I reluctantly had to tear myself away.

My kids were fast asleep when I finally got home. I was so tired, but I knew that I wouldn't get much sleep that night. I was feeling a little strange. I didn't know how I should feel about Rocco and our new relationship anymore. What were the rules? Would we continue to have sex with each other, or did we have an affair and now it was over? Could we see other people, or were we exclusive to one another? Obviously it didn't apply to me as I really wasn't seeing anyone, but what about Rocco? How did I feel about him being with other women? I already admitted to feeling a little jealous about his dead wife, but what about all of the gorgeous women that he sleeps with? I just wanted an uncomplicated relationship. How stupid and naïve of me to ever think that a relationship that involved sex could ever be uncomplicated.

And what about Alex? I wondered if my feelings for him should be different now that I'd had an intimate relationship with Rocco. When I saw Alex at the dinner party and we spoke, well, those old emotions were still there. However, I was not certain if those emotions were genuine. I can be very stubborn, and I'm just way too loyal for my own good. *Do I love Alex, or am I stubbornly hanging on to the idea of being with my perfect man?*

All I ever really wanted was to feel desirable

and to get some affection. Oh yeah, and I'm sure it's obvious that I just really needed to get properly fucked at least once before I die. Well, thanks to Rocco, that finally happened.

24

Honesty Is So Over-Rated

I spent the next day pretty much working on my
column. I got a lot of work done considering
that I hadn't slept much the night before.
Oddly enough, I didn't even feel tired. The only
way that I could describe how I felt is to describe
it as that feeling that you have after you've just
gotten a really nice haircut. You know that feeling,
when you look good so you feel good, and you get a
lot of attention from people as you walk past them.
I guess I felt revitalized.

Rocco called me late in the morning. He was
busy at work and he was going to have a pretty
heavy workload for the rest of the week. He made a
point of telling me this. Why was he telling me this

information? Was he feeling tired of me already and made up an excuse so that he wouldn't have to see me again so soon? Or did he feel like now that we have an intimate relationship, he would have to apprise me of his whereabouts at all times?

But Rocco showed up at my house that day.

"Rocco? What a surprise?" I was standing at the entrance door and moved to the side so that he could enter, but he just stood there.

"Aren't you going to invite me in, Briana?"

"What do you think I'm doing, Rocco? Do you need to hear me say the words inviting you into my home? What are you, a vampire or something?"

"Yeah, sure, *a vampire*. And I wanna suck on something, alright, but it's not your blood!" Rocco winked at me, a devilish grin on his face.

"I thought that you had a lot of work to do."

"I do, but I wanted to, umm, I just wanted to make sure that you had something to eat." We sat in my kitchen and ate lunch together.

I couldn't help but think how out of place Rocco looked in my small kitchen. His kitchen was big, and the appliances were top of the line. My kitchen was functional, but no luxuries here. It was beginning to look worn, used, and outdated. New appliances weren't exactly a priority in my life. I know that Rocco noticed how unattractive my appliances were, because when I caught him looking at them intently, he merely said that they looked "interesting." He loves quality and every-thing has to be top of the line with him, but he's also very polite and kind. He wouldn't say anything that might hurt my feelings—intentionally.

"Are you feeling OK, Rocco? Maybe you shouldn't have gone to work today."

"I'm good, Briana. Isn't this chicken good? This place near my office makes the best grilled chicken!"

"What are you doing here, Rocco? You're acting weird, and we agreed that we wouldn't act weird, remember?"

"Have you been in touch with Alex? Weren't you supposed to meet with him sometime this week?"

"Yes, I told him that I would have dinner with him, but I haven't spoken to him yet."

Rocco stopped eating and just looked at me for a few seconds. "I don't want you to meet with him."

"And why not? I already told him that I would meet him."

"Because there's absolutely no reason for you to meet with him. If he has something to say to you, well, he can say it over the phone."

"Tell me why you don't want me to meet with him."

"Because you'll meet with him, he'll be all charming, and you'll fall into his arms."

"What if I need strong arms to hold me tight, Rocco? You told me so many times that I need a big, strong man to help me out. Maybe you're right."

Rocco looked at me, and within seconds his piercing stare turned into a smoldering one. He came over to me and squatted in front of my chair, taking my hands in his. "Aren't my arms strong enough for you, Briana?"

I wanted to laugh but knew that it would piss him off, so I bit my lip instead. "Rocco, your arms are so strong, and I love being in them."

"So isn't this enough for you, Briana? Aren't I enough for you?"

I couldn't believe my ears! "*You are more than enough*, and any woman would be lucky to be in your arms. Rocco, what are you really saying?"

"I don't know. What I do know is that I don't want you to be intimate with Alex. I can give you everything that you need, at least as far as intimacy goes."

"Is it just Alex, or is it OK for me to see other men?"

"I know that you're not the type to go from one man to another, Briana. You wouldn't degrade yourself in that way."

"I see." I really didn't see at all. "And what about you, Rocco? What about all the beautiful women that come in and out of your life? *Can I give you everything that you need, at least as far as intimacy goes?* Or is it OK for you, Rocco, to let other women fall asleep in your bed, in your strong arms?"

"Don't be ridiculous, Briana. I don't let anyone sleep in my bed."

"You let me sleep in your bed."

"Look, this is new to me, OK. All I know right now is that I like being with you, Briana. And when

I'm not with you, well, all I can think about is the next time that I'll be with you. You're truly in my life now, in every way, and I don't want anyone hurting what's mine."

"What's yours! Are you kidding me?"

"I'm not using the right words, but you know what I mean."

"Are you going to *fuck around with* other women, Rocco? Or am *I* enough for *you*?"

Rocco took my thumb and put it in his mouth. He sucked on it gently before actually answering my question. "How could I be with other women when all I want is to be with you?" He picked me up and wrapped my legs around him while my arms went around his neck. He held me real close to him and grabbed my ass. "This is what I've wanted to do since you left me last night." He slid his tongue inside my mouth and we kissed, hungrily. We made our way over to the sofa, and I still had my legs wrapped around him as we sat down.

"What are we doing, Rocco?"

"I don't know. I don't think that either of us is really ready to define what our relationship is, or to commit to anything major. But I do know that I like having you in my life. I like that we're good friends. I also admit that what I feel for you is more than just friendship, but I'm not ready to think about anything beyond that."

I totally understood what he was saying, but I couldn't help feeling a little disappointed and maybe even a little hurt by it. Maybe I really was expecting him to profess his undying love for me. I'm so pathetic. I just really want someone to love me, deeply and passionately. I got off of Rocco and sat next to him.

"I want to be honest with you, Briana, because I do care so much about you."

Honesty? Why does everyone feel a need to be honest with me? It's so fuckin' over-rated! But I guess it's better than being led on and lied to.

"I guess I appreciate your honesty, and I care about you too. Don't ever stop being honest with me, OK?"

He turned my face toward him with his finger, and then he made to kiss me. I'm not sure if it was because I was hurt or disappointed, but I just couldn't let him kiss me anymore. I was a little angry too, but I couldn't let Rocco know how I felt. What was I expecting, anyway? Did I think that I could let him forget about his dead wife just because he slept with me? I guess maybe deep down inside I did think that.

I've been through too much in my life, so I just couldn't let myself ruin a good friendship. It seems that I'm just so needy these days, because as much as I needed to get a *proper fucking*, I also really need a good friend in my life. So I just put a smile on my face and lied to Rocco. Besides, he looked like he'd just lost his best friend. I wanted to make sure that things were still good between us.

"Hey, Rocco, thanks so much for coming by and for lunch. I don't want to be rude, but I have so much work to do. I have to finish writing my article by the end of the day and I'm not even close to being done."

Rocco looked at me with narrowed eyes, but then he just got up and ran his hand through his hair.

"OK, honey. I'll go for now. I actually have a lot of work to do myself. Can I see you tonight?"

"I'm sorry, Rocco, but I need to spend some time with my kids. They'll be getting back from school in a couple of hours, and I just want to cook a nice dinner and spend some quality time with them." I could see that he looked a little suspicious, as if he didn't really buy what I was saying. My pride made me go on. I reached for his hand and held it in mine. "Raincheck?"

"Sure." I walked him out and we kissed briefly on the mouth. Just like a real couple. I really did want to be with my kids. I also needed some quality time with myself. The smart thing to do was to try and stay away from any complications in my life. Somehow, I only seemed to attract complications.

As I watched Rocco drive away, I just felt so confused. I liked Rocco and I liked being with him. He was fun to be with and he made me feel good. Of course, I also felt a little shitty because I was growing more and more resentful of his dead wife, and jealous of the love that they'd shared.

25

Loins on Fire

Rocco drove away feeling a little empty, confused, and plenty frustrated. Just what was going on with him? His need to see Briana today made him cut short an important meeting with a client, and he showed up at her doorstep with the excuse of wanting to have lunch with her. He laughed to himself when he thought about how he stumbled to her front door. There was so much damage to her driveway, and it was in need of major repairs. He made a mental note to do something about that.

It felt good to see her and to hold her in his arms. He missed her already. He just really liked being with her. It made things complicated.

Life was so much simpler without the need to be with someone. Was there room in his life and in his heart for someone other than Angela? Could he love again? Could he love another woman? Would Angela understand?

Was he setting himself up for more pain? If he allowed himself to love again, well, he was also allowing the possibility of excruciating pain back into his life. He couldn't bear the thought of losing someone that he loved again.

If he allowed love back into his life, would that be a betrayal of Angela? He meant it when he told Angela that he would love her forever. He still did love Angela so much, and he missed her.

Rocco was back at his office, sitting at his desk, but work was far from his mind. "What am I doing? Why am I looking for trouble? Do I really need this in my life?" He was rubbing his scar so hard that he started to feel the skin around it sting a little. He made his way over to the couch, slipped off his shoes, and plopped his long, heavy body down on it. He was facing the wall with the collage of Angela's pictures. A "shrine," Briana had called it.

God, I miss Angela, he thought to himself. He missed hearing her laugh, talking to her, hugging her, feeling her in his arms and waking up with her in the morning. She was so precious to him. How could he betray that by loving someone else?

"How could I let this happen?"

What could he do? One thing he knew for sure

was that he couldn't turn away from Briana now. He didn't want to, but more importantly, he knew that he just couldn't do it. His heart was one thing, and it tormented him on so many levels. It was his heart and guilt that kept him from committing to any woman other than Angela. But his body was an entirely different monster. He felt like a teenage boy again, with uncontrollable raging hormones. *A horny teenage boy!* Except now the big tits and ass that were always so readily available to him could no longer satiate his hunger. There was a hunger and a fire deep within his loins that only Briana could seem to satisfy.

26

How Can I Thank You Enough?

The music was blazing. There was a big band playing jazz music. It was a night club, and everyone seemed to be having such a good time. The look of the place was so Deco. What a strange feeling to be watching this go on. The women were dressed in beautiful twenties-style fashion. Everyone was dancing. They were doing the Charleston!

"Alex? What are you doing here?" He didn't answer me. He didn't even seem to hear me. He was so engrossed in a conversation with a woman. He *was holding her hand and smiling at her. And he was looking at her with so much love in his eyes. The woman reached forward and kissed him.*

What was he doing here, and why was he kissing this woman?

"Alex?"

He didn't hear me, but the woman in his arms did. She turned to face me.

What the fuck! The hair was different, and the dress that she was wearing was definitely something that I would've picked out if it was the roaring twenties. But her face, well, it was me. She looked exactly like me.

"Who are you? Do I know you?" I asked the woman, but she didn't answer me. She just smiled and looked at me with a knowing look. It was so eerie.

She then pointed to the door behind me. "What? Do you want me to leave?"

"Mommy! There's someone at the door. Get up, Mommy."

"What? What is it, sweetheart?" Marco was standing by my bed, pulling on my arm. "There's someone at the door, Mommy. Didn't you hear the doorbell?"

"OK, my love. I'll get up. Where's your sister?"

"She's sleeping in her bedroom."

Good God. It was 6 a.m. Who the fuck was at

my door at this early hour?

"Please go wake up Elisa and get ready for school."

What a strange dream I had. It certainly wasn't my first strange dream involving Alex. I had had many of them, although they did become a little stranger over time.

They always left me feeling a little confused, anxious, weirded out. They were strange because they didn't really feel like dreams sometimes. It felt more like I was looking in on someone's private life. I was a voyeur in my own life. The dreams always felt real. Like I really experienced what I was seeing in my dream. It was all so familiar.

From the very beginning when I first met Alex, I always had that strong sensation of knowing him intimately. His voice was so familiar to me, and I immediately felt a deep connection with him. It was these deep feelings of having a strong connection with him that got me into trouble in the beginning as I allowed myself to speak to him and text him inappropriately. *So, what is up with that?*

I answered my front door to find about four men working on my driveway. "Good morning," I said as I tightened the belt of my robe around my waist.

"Good morning, madame. My name is Guy. Mr. Di Re hired us to work on your driveway and landscaping."

Rocco! Of course he did.

"What exactly did he hire you to do?"

"We will redo your driveway in unistone, and we will redo the landscaping. Sorry to ring the doorbell so early, but we didn't want to begin working without speaking to you first. It'll take us a couple of days to get the job done, but I promise you that it'll be beautiful.

"OK. Thank you, Mr. Guy, and please let me know if you or the other men need anything."

How typical of Rocco. He's such a control freak. I should have been offended, upset, or embarrassed. But I wasn't any of those things. My whole house could use a face-lift. A new driveway would look great. Thank you, Rocco!

Later on that morning, my doorbell rang again. Beautiful new appliances had been delivered to my home. You guessed it: Rocco! I was stunned! Is this what being a "kept" woman feels like? Was I a kept woman? I hope not, because it has such an ugly ring to it, although I have to say that I was thrilled with the new appliances. They were beautiful, stainless steel of course, and huge! They looked like the appliances that you see on cooking shows on television.

But why was Rocco doing this for me? Did my home look so awful to him that he had to fix it? Or was this some kind of payment for my "sexual services"? If I didn't know how generous and kind Rocco was, then I could actually believe it. But Rocco is good and generous and old-fashioned. He did this for me because he cares about me, and if anyone should be getting any type of compensation for sexual services rendered, well, you know that I'm the one who should be paying him! He's the one that broke through the cobwebs that had formed around my lonely, forgotten womanhood. He made me feel like a sexual, vibrant woman again.

I didn't know how to respond to this latest act of generosity from Rocco. I should've known better than to worry about what to do with him, as I knew that with him I could just be honest.

Once the delivery guys left, I phoned Rocco to thank him. It barely rang once before he picked up.

"I was wondering when you'd call." Rocco bypassed "hello" with an amused drawl in his voice.

"What did you do, Rocco?"

"Don't you like any of it?"

"Of course I do. But--"

He interrupted me, as I knew he would. "No buts about it, sweetheart."

"Did my home look so ugly to you that you immediately had to make changes to meet your standards?"

"Don't be stupid! Your home is just fine. But I know that you like good things and I'm lucky enough to have the money to buy nice things for you. Briana, it's just money, and if I can use it to bring some happiness into your life, then it works for me."

"You're so generous, so kind to me."

"It makes me feel good to help you."

"Help me? Like I'm a charitable case..."

"And there you go being stupid again! Listen to me, I have the money and I want to spend it in the way that makes me happy. Now stop your foolish, childish behavior and tell me how you're going to thank me for giving you lavish gifts." He was laughing again.

"Of course, true generosity means never having to say thank you."

"What? Oh no, honey, I want you to thank me. It's the polite thing to do, of course."

"So how should I thank you, then?"

"Be creative, and remember, make it good and worth my while."

"Seriously?"

Rocco was laughing but finally said, "No, I'm not serious. I just want you to be happy. Can you have supper with me tonight?"

"Yes." My response was given before he had a chance to finish his sentence. I really wanted to see him. If he enjoyed giving me things, then I have to say that it really turned me on to have someone be so generous with me. Nobody had ever treated me this way before. Nobody ever cared enough about me to simply want to find ways to make me happy.

"Where are we eating? Are we going out, or do you want to eat in?"

"How about I come over with some food and we all eat together? *You know*, me, you, *the kids...*"

Huh! He wanted to get close to my kids. I guess I was OK with it, although it was surprising to me to realize that I wasn't too ready just yet. Having a good man around my kids is not a bad idea. My kids, especially Marco, really miss having a male figure around. A father figure to play hockey with, kick the soccer ball with in the backyard... I tried so hard to make it work with Peter, all those years in a miserable marriage, for my children. Kids really do want a mom and a dad that live together, that do things together, and, of course, that love each other. My kids deserve the perfect family life, and I am filled with so much guilt for failing to give it to them. I was a little confused about what to do, but one thing is for sure when it comes to my kids, taking it slowly and cautiously is best.

"Rocco, I'd love for you to get to know my kids better, but maybe coming over for supper tonight will be a little much for them." *A little much for me too.* "Where my kids are concerned, I'd like to take it slowly. You know, maybe we can meet at the ice-cream shop and get a cone one night, then maybe go bowling the next time, and then maybe go for a burger, and lead up to coming over for dinner."

"Bri, they already know who I am."

"Yes, but they know you as someone that I work with, not really as a friend of mine and certainly not as someone that I'm *very close* to. Are you offended? Do you understand? I didn't hurt your feelings, did I?"

"No, no, sweetheart. I guess I understand. I'm sorry. I just feel really anxious to get to know Elisa and Marco. But you're right, honey. I don't want to do anything that will upset them in any way. You know best where your kids are concerned."

"OK, Rocco, so I'll see you tonight. It's really nice out. Can we eat at your place, *al fresco*?" He has such a beautiful home, and such a lovely patio. It's much prettier than any restaurant could ever be, not to mention more private. "I'll bring the food."

"Don't be ridiculous. OK, we'll eat at home, but I'll take care of the food. See you later."

"See you later."

"Um, Briana?"

"Yes?"

"I look forward to seeing you."

"I can't wait to see you, Rocco." *And I can't wait to kiss you, melt in your arms, and smell your sexy, manly scent...*

I took my time to get ready for my *date* with Rocco. I paid special attention to my skin. I shaved, exfoliated, creamed, and perfumed all of my *strategic* areas. It's definitely a different sensation to get ready for a date when you know that you'll probably "get lucky." *No granny panties tonight!*

27

I Already Shaved, After All...

Rocco was out on the patio barbecuing some steaks for our meal. I found myself once again standing in front of his late wife's portrait, just looking into the gentle eyes of the woman who owned Rocco's heart.

"I slept with your husband, although you probably already know that, don't you?" I was speaking to her portrait. What a strange feeling. "Do you mind?" I continued. It felt a little like adultery, a little wrong. But she's dead. Rocco and Angela aren't together because she died, not because they stopped loving each other. They would still be together had it not been for Angela's tragic death. So, is it adultery? She's dead, but Rocco's heart still belongs to her.

She seemed to be looking back at me with a knowing smile on her face. She knows, and she's fine with it. My relationship with Rocco doesn't bother her, because she knows that he'll never love me in the way that he loves her.

"Briana? Where are you, sweetheart? Come out on the patio, please?"

He fixed us a couple of drinks. He knew that I had been looking at his late wife's portrait, but he didn't mention it. *Should I mention it?* I wondered. *Don't think so.* Why would I ruin a perfectly good evening? Maybe I would mention it after sex. *Oh come on! I shaved and all.*

Was I expecting too much? *Shouldn't I expect too much?* Why can't I just be happy with Rocco and with the way that things are? I can't change the fact that he was married to the love of his life. Why do *I* even want to be the love of *his* life? I guess it's because I've never been anyone's true love.

Rocco's uncle Sal phoned while we were eating our meal. It was clear by the look on Rocco's face that something was wrong, although he was trying to hide it. "Uncle Sal, I have it all under control. Don't you worry about it, OK." He looked at me with a strange smile on his face, a forced smile. "Sure, I'll let you know if I need your help. I'll call you tomorrow."

"Are you ready for dessert, Briana?"

"Dessert?" He was avoiding my inevitable questioning, so I knew that it was bad. "What was that about, Rocco?"

"Nothing." He smiled and reached across the table to grab my hand, then leaned over and kissed the inside of my hand.

"Don't say that it's nothing, Rocco. You're scaring me!"

"*Easy, honey.* Don't overreact!"

"What! Don't be like that, Rocco. I won't have it! Now tell me what's wrong, or I'm so out of here!"

Rocco took a deep breath. He filled our glasses with more wine. He finally spoke.

"Somehow the Marconi's found out about my book." That's the family that Rocco is writing about. "They don't want it to be published."

"And?"

"And I couldn't care less about what those fuckers want. Come on, everyone knows what a corrupt family they are. It's no surprise to anyone. Such hypocrites! Besides, my book is fiction, and 'any resemblance to actual persons, living or dead, is entirely coincidental.' Right?" He said it while rolling his eyes and laughing to himself.

"What else? How do you know that the Marconi's came to learn of your book?"

"They may have sent me a few messages."

"Oh my God, Rocco! What did they do?"

"They sent me a few threatening phone messages and, uh--" He hesitated for a few moments.

"What? What!!"

"The windshield of my car was completely smashed, and the tires were cut. They left a burnt copy of a book on my front seat. What a bunch of idiots. Oh yeah, how symbolic, now I'm really *scared*!"

"Don't do that! You should take threats very seriously! Did you call the police?"

"No, because they don't scare me. Look, don't worry about it, OK. They're just cowards, and I have it under control. Enough now."

"Rocco, tell me why you can't let this go. I know that there's more to it, and you owe me the truth."

I could see that my words made an impact on him. He took a few moments, as if to collect his thoughts, and then he looked at me with a pained look in his eyes.

"The man that raped and killed my mother was Marconi's nephew and lawyer. That monster was free to terrorize so many people, and he was untouchable because he was under the protection of the Marconi criminal family."

"Oh, Rocco, this is really personal for you."

"Damn right it is!" His words were dripping with hate.

"This is too dangerous, Rocco! You need to stop this."

That's when Rocco seemed to relax again. He looked at me with a grin on his face. "Don't worry about it, I got this."

"*But* Rocco..."

"Yes, get your *butt* over here, right now." He completely ignored my protests, and dismissed my fears.

"I'm scared, Rocco."

"Hey, hey, don't be. I'm a badass, remember?" He laughed, got up, and came over to my side of the table.

"No, you're not a badass. You are the kindest and most gentle person that I have ever met. You pretend to be tough, but you're not."

"What! Come on, honey, now you're hurting my feelings." He looked at me with an exaggerated hurt expression on his face. *On his beautiful, strong face...*

"This," I grabbed his face with both of my hands, "is all the dessert that I'm in the mood for right now."

I ran my tongue along his beautiful, sexy, sensual lips.

He pulled me up into his strong arms. My legs wrapped around his body, and my arms around his neck. He held onto my ass and was squeezing gently. But I wasn't in the mood for gentle squeezing. I was in the mood for some rougher loving tonight.

I was rubbing my already very wet pussy against his rock hard cock. I kept on kissing him and licking him. He was just so delicious. And my need to suck his cock was getting stronger and stronger.

"Let's get naked, Rocco. I wanna suck you now."

28

Just Let Me Go Down on You Already!

She never ceases to amaze me. Briana is so sweet, and so passionate! She really doesn't have a problem telling me just how much she wants to fuck me. I can see how much she wants me. It's in her eyes when she looks at me. I can feel how much she wants me. It's in the way that she touches me and holds onto me. It's definitely in the way that she grabs hold of my cock. It's in the way that she strokes it and runs her tongue along the length of it. It's like she's really enjoying it, and I know that it's really me that she's enjoying, and that fuckin' turns me on. And her soft, guttural groans! Just hearing her voice makes me hard. I'm starting to obsess about her. I think about her all of the time, and it's not just because I want to be in her. I want to be *with* her. There's really no turning back now.

"Rocco, aren't you enjoying this? You seem to be a million miles away."

"*I am SOO enjoying this.* And *I am* miles away. You take me far away, to places that I've never been to before!"

She kept sucking my cock. I had to constantly fight the urge to let her take my entire cock inside her mouth. I could tell that she's insecure because she often slightly hesitates, but it only makes me want to take her and make love to her in the way that she deserves to be loved. And I know that it's her desire to please me that enables her to be brave and follow her instincts, and it makes her so incredibly hot. *God! What is she doing to me!* I needed to stop thinking so much, and I needed her to stop before I came in her mouth.

I slowly removed my cock from inside her mouth. Was that fear in her eyes, or was it just a little confusion that I saw there? I smiled at her, and she instantly returned my smile. I pulled her up to me. I kissed her mouth and realized that I could actually taste myself on her lips. What's even more surprising is that it didn't turn me off. It actually got me harder for her. I grabbed and squeezed her breasts, and licked one nipple and then sucked on it. I did the same with her other perfect breast. I ran my tongue along her stomach, moving downwards, toward her hot, wet pussy. I wanted to lick her tender, swollen bud. My tongue was thirsting for her, and I got to lick her vagina before she pulled me away.

"Don't," was all that she said, breathless.

I continued on, ignoring her.

"Please, don't do that."

"I want to. You took care of me, so let me do you. OK, baby?"

"No, please, I don't want that." She tried to pull herself away from my mouth.

Unbelievable! That's one thing that I just didn't get about this woman. On a number of occasions, she stopped me from going down on her. She said that she just didn't want it. She was so obviously uncomfortable with it. For a woman who can suck my cock with such passion and fuck me with such enthusiasm, she sure is a little bit of a prude when it came to receiving oral sex. Eventually she's gonna have to get over it. Her pussy is mine, and I take good care of what's mine. She'll come around soon enough.

Our positions shifted so that she was now sitting on top of my cock. I was lying back and could see her beautiful tits bounce with every rocking motion of my cock sliding in and out of her pussy. She was actually moving up and down on me, taking my cock in as she slid down on me, and then taking it out as she slid upwards. She was groaning as she grabbed onto her swollen tits, squeezing, and looking at me with those hungry eyes of hers. She wanted me. She was enjoying fucking me. I leaned forward and grabbed onto her ass. I brought her all the way down on me. My whole cock was inside her now, and she looked at me with such satisfaction on her face. She was loving it, and I was so ready to explode my load inside her.

"I'm gonna come, baby! Are you ready for me?"

"Yes, come now. Come for me, now."

We just lay there, side by side, breathing heavily and looking at each other in the eyes. It took us a while to catch our breaths. It felt nice being next to her like this. It felt so satisfying, so relaxing, and so right.

"Rocco?" She ran her fingertip along my lips. "Didn't you mention something about dessert?"

I couldn't help but laugh. "Yeah, sure, honey. I'll go get it and I'll be right back."

29

Tell Me about Your Childhood

"**W**hat's your name?" I asked the soldier as I helped him take his medication. His leg had to be amputated. He told me that he had a wife and baby waiting for him back home, but he was in no hurry to get back to them now. He felt like he'd let his country down as well as his family because he was injured. This brave soldier lost his leg, and he's worried that he let his country down? He's so lucky to be alive. The doctor said that he came so close to losing his life and that he wasn't out of the woods yet.

The doctor needed my help with a patient who was brought in this morning and who was at the other end from where I was currently working.

I slowly woke up as I was making my way toward the doctor. Alex! Alex was the doctor in my dream! *Good God in heaven!* Another dream. These dreams of mine were way too active. They were making me exhausted.

I didn't stay the night at Rocco's. I left shortly after we made love. I can't just forget that I have kids to take care of, so sleepovers can't be the usual for me. I have to say, though, that it was really hard to leave Rocco last night. He is such a good lover. I just love the way he holds me, and grabs me, and kisses me, and fucks me. It feels so good to be in a relationship with a man who wants to have sex with me just as often as I want to with him. I never had that before.

I would've thought that all that lovemaking would've guaranteed me a good night's sleep, but I was wrong. I had such a restless night. It's because I kept dreaming about Alex. It's not so much dreaming about Alex that I find disturbing, as much as the nature of the dreams.

My dreams are just so very familiar to me. They feel like déjà vu. In my dream last night, Alex was a doctor, but it was during some war period. The scene could've been out of a war movie. I was with Alex, and I worked with him. I think I may have been a nurse or some kind of caregiver, because I was always with him, assisting him.

Even in my dreams I'm an underachiever! Why wasn't I the doctor!

I loved Alex in my dream. Although the dream was about the two of us helping wounded soldiers, there was no doubt that we were a couple. At one point in the dream, Alex and I were alone by the side of a big tent, and he kissed me on the lips and told me that he loved me. We were definitely a couple, and in love with one another.

I always have a hard time getting back to sleep after I have one of my dreams about Alex. My dreams are becoming more and more intense. I'm always left feeling a sense of loss that makes me very anxious, confused, and a little sad. My connection to Alex is just so strong. Maybe once I tell Alex that I'm now with Rocco, I'll stop dreaming about him.

I managed to put off meeting with Alex, but I really can't put it off any longer. He said that he needs to speak with me. I know that he feels badly about how we left things off the last time that we saw each other. But why does he want to see me so badly now? Rocco thinks that Alex wants me, physically wants me, and he doesn't like it one bit. I don't know what to think.

I do know that Alex is still in my heart. That hasn't changed for me. But now I have Rocco to think about. Rocco, well, he's my rock.

When I think about Alex, I almost feel a little shy and gauche. He makes me want to be a better person, which is usually a good thing. Everyone should want to continually better themselves. I want Alex to see me as attractive, intelligent, and well spoken. I want him to see me as successful. I want him to approve of me, and I wouldn't want him to be embarrassed to be seen with me or to tell anyone that we are a couple. *A little exhausting, yes?* And after the marriage that I had and the verbal abuse from so many over the years, I never want to feel inadequate again. I need to be happy and comfortable in my own skin. I want to be loved and wanted just the way that I am.

It's a little different with Rocco. I don't need to impress him. I think he likes me the way that I am. He doesn't mind if my hair is a little messy, he actually likes it when it is. I feel free with Rocco. I don't have to pretend with him. I can openly tell him that I want to fuck him, and he's just fine with that. No games, no judgment. I believe that he loves me. Well, as much as he can ever love anyone again. Maybe love is a strong word, but I know that he wants me and he makes me feel so sexy. He's so strong and protective, passionate, an amazing lover, and he's just so fuckin' hot. He makes me feel like I'm *his,* like I belong to him. And strangely enough, it doesn't bother me in the least. I like it, and it turns me on.

However, I owe it to Alex to tell him that I'm with Rocco now. I don't want him to find out some other way. Rocco and Alex are often at the same events. I will be joining Rocco from now on at social events, and I want to *openly* accompany him.

The psychic came highly recommended. My neighbor said that she had used her services when she had a hard time dealing with the death of her husband. I was skeptical at first. Why a psychic? However, I just can't get over the feeling that there is more to my relationship with Alex. I felt this way even when he was basically a stranger to me, way back when he operated on my mom. I remember looking into his eyes and feeling like I knew him. And what about the weird dreams that I've been having about Alex lately? And no, I'm not referring to my "wet dreams." My dreams are so vivid and real. So I figured, what do I have to lose? At the very least, it should be entertaining.

Magda, the psychic, or "intuitive therapist" as she called herself, lives in an artsy neighborhood not too far from the bustling streets of downtown Montreal. She works out of her home. I was expecting to find a very flamboyant, colorful woman wearing long, baggy, bright clothing, with a *foulard* wrapped around her head and her face slathered with heavy makeup. I guess I was thinking of the type of woman that you would find at a psychic booth of a carnival.

The woman that I met with couldn't have been more different from what I expected. She was wearing a tan-colored pant suit, and her hair was dark and short, no makeup. She had a very soft-spoken, sweet voice, and there was just something about her that was so calming.

I sat on a very comfortable, soft leather black sofa. Now, lying on a sofa talking about my feelings is exactly what I expected! Magda asked me to talk about what compelled me to finally see a "professional." Although she wasn't interested in my childhood yet, she wanted me to speak about some of the experiences leading to my decision to meet with her. Don't psychotherapists always want to know about your childhood first? Are psychics— sorry, *intuitive therapists*—even considered to be psychotherapists? *Whatever.*

So I told her about how I felt when I first met Alex. I told her how I felt such a deep connection with him, from the very first time that I saw him when he introduced himself as my mom's lung doctor. How I looked into his eyes, basically the eyes of a stranger, and I felt like I knew him intimately. I explained how my dreams felt so real and how I felt that I had actually experienced what I had seen in my dreams.

Magda just listened and took notes. She didn't seem to be judging me, although I really sounded like a love-sick schoolgirl. I sure as hell didn't sound like a grown woman, a mother nonetheless! But you know, it actually feels good to talk about your personal strange thoughts or experiences with someone who doesn't personally know you. I'm sure that I'm not the first nut that she's met. Hey, I'm probably not the nuttiest one either!

By the end of my time with her, close to one hour and a half later, Magda told me that she would like to explore some of my experiences in a little more detail. She did explain that some of what I was describing sounded like past-life memories emerging. Maybe I felt this strong connection to Alex because I did know him in a past life. Apparently, it's very common to travel through different lifetimes with the same groups of souls. God, I hope that's not true, because there are some "souls" that I've met here in this life that I sure don't want to be around in my next life, wherever that may be. But it sure does feel like it with Alex.

Magda said that she would like to guide me through a past-life regression experience. I read about those, and although it does interest me, I'm not too crazy about it for myself. But really, what do I have to lose? So, I made an appointment to see her in two weeks. Apparently, there's a lot of demand for psychics these days and it's a little tough to get an appointment.

Although I really wasn't surprised to hear the psychic mention "past lives," I still was a little weirded out by it. It just felt so strange. All of it felt strange, but then again, a lot about my life has felt surreal ever since I first met the great Dr. Ferrante.

It almost feels like knowing for certain that there is more or something else out there besides the physical world that we currently live in. Of course I don't really know anything for sure, but

I sure as hell feel like I do. It's like I'm a character in a science fiction movie. Except this is not a movie. Maybe we can think of our life as a movie. Different phases in our lives are different scenes, and the end of the movie marks the end of our life. As with every movie, we enjoy certain parts and may find other scenes a little dull. Sometimes we need to cry. If we're lucky, we need to laugh more often than not. Once the movie is over, did we enjoy it, or did we feel like we wasted our time? Do we then move on to the next movie? Are we all but actors, and is the world truly our stage? OK, I'm in a pretty bad state when I start quoting Shakespeare!

Magda mentioned that we do often move through different lifetimes with the same groups of souls. Maybe we are but actors hoping to get cast in the next great movie. It's not uncommon for actors to have worked together in several different movies.

You may have understood by now that I am a spiritual person. I believe that there is a higher power out there. I believe in God, and yes, I do love Jesus, although I'm not the type to have it stated on a bumper sticker on my car.

I do believe that our soul is sent here for a reason, and that we need to see it through to the end, whether our journey is easy or even excruciating. It's so hard to understand why some people have to experience such unheard of pain. It often makes me cry to think of it. But again, I do believe that there is a reason for it, although we may not understand it.

But once my journey is over, I don't want to stick around for a double feature. The only thing keeping me going is my belief that after this is over, well, I can go back home to God, where it's safe and where there is no pain.

So, what if we need to stick around for yet another movie? What will the new script have in store for us? Will we find more of the same? Will we have different experiences, more pain, or, if we're lucky, more happiness? They say that we're either lucky in love or in cards. I've never gambled, but I can only assume that I'm lucky in cards because I sure as hell haven't been too lucky in the love department.

Did I know Alex in a previous life? It feels like it to me. I don't think that I simply knew him. Surely there are many characters in a movie, including extras and people that work behind the scenes. They don't really touch our lives though. Very few people do. I think that I must have had a great intimate connection to Alex for the feeling to have endured through different lifetimes. Oh my God! I know it sounds crazy, and yet it feels so right. Dare I say it? Yes, I do believe that Alex is my soul mate.

30

Not in This Lifetime

Inoticed that I was holding my breath, sitting in a booth at the local deli. Elisa was seated next to me, and Marco sat next to Rocco across the table just facing us. It was so hard to enjoy the smoked meat sandwiches laid out in front of us when I couldn't even breathe properly. Rocco wanted to meet my kids, and he kept asking me to arrange an appropriate date for us all. So we arranged for Rocco to coincidentally come to the deli near my home when we just happened to be having lunch there, and, well, it was the polite thing to do to invite him to join us.

Not only were my kids not fazed in the least, but they seemed to really enjoy Rocco's company.

It's easy to be drawn to Rocco because he's such a force of nature. He's so big and strong, yet kind and gentle. You automatically feel protected around him. And he's really funny. He acts so silly and goofy around my kids. He really would've made a great dad.

So after our meal, we went home. Rocco and I decided that it was probably best if he just went to his own home, but not without a promise to Marco that he would help him build a great tree house. Marco asked me for a tree house on so many occasions. Of course, I didn't know how to help him with this. How typical that Rocco would be the one that my son would turn to. It's like I said, there's something about Rocco that makes you feel that he could do anything. He's like a superhero!

I agreed to meet with Alex at the Foundation's office. I couldn't meet him for supper at a restaurant, and I didn't want him to come over to my house. I wanted it to be as professional as possible.

I was already at the office, pretending to work, when he came in. He stood by the door and simply watched me for a few seconds, although it felt like many long, excruciating minutes had gone by. When I just couldn't take it anymore, I looked up at him and acted surprised to see him there. He was in his scrubs, *damn it*, and he did look tired, but nonetheless so sexy and good-looking.

He smiled at me, and then he came in closer. "You're such a sight for sore eyes. You look amazing."

My heart was pounding in my ears, and my tongue felt swollen in my mouth. "So do you," I said honestly, and just barely loud enough for him to hear me.

"I've been operating for the past nine hours!"

"Like I said, you look amazing." I just can't keep my mouth shut. *Yeah, honesty is so over-rated.*

Alex looked at me with that sexy smile of his. "Thanks for meeting me, Briana. But why don't we go over to my place. I'll change and then we'll go grab a bite to eat."

"I can't, Alex. Please, just tell me why you needed to speak with me in person. I don't have much time. I need to get back to my kids."

"Or is it Rocco that you need to get back to?"

I was a little surprised to learn that Alex knew about Rocco and me, but I guess I really shouldn't have been. Alex isn't stupid.

"Look, Briana, I understand how you could have turned to Rocco. He's a good guy. And he probably would be the right guy for you, if I wasn't in the picture."

"But you're not in the picture, Alex. Remember? The best you could offer me was an affair."

Alex winced at my biting words. "You're right. I was an idiot, Briana. I didn't know what I wanted. I have so much on my plate; I just didn't want to set myself up for failure. I failed once before, and I don't want to again."

I couldn't help feeling a little angry over his words, a little flabbergasted, and very upset. All I wanted was to feel a little love from someone, anyone in my life. I wanted to feel a little desired. I still didn't know what he really wanted from me.

"What are you saying, Alex? Actually, forget it. It doesn't matter anymore."

"When I learned about you and Rocco, I was devastated. I felt such a loss. How could I let you get away?"

"So what's your problem, Alex? Why are we here? You still didn't tell me."

"My problem is that I don't want to lose you to Rocco. I need you."

"You're so full of it, Alex. You still won't say it. You just don't want to lose me to Rocco. You don't want to 'lose'! You don't want to feel like someone else has more appeal than you do. You don't give a damn about me. You don't want me."

"I'm not used to saying these words. But don't get me wrong; I do want you. It's not just about losing you to Rocco. I don't want you with any man. I want you with me. I knew it and I felt our connection from the very beginning. When I learned about you and Rocco, I realized that I couldn't let you go."

"This is crazy, Alex. And it's too late."

I dreamt about this on so many occasions. I remember being a young girl, reading my beloved Harlequin romance books, and imagining that I was the girl on the cover being embraced by a strong, gorgeous man who would fight for my love. Is my present reality really what I dreamt about all those years ago? I guess I do have two strong, gorgeous men who claimed to want me. After living without love for so long, do I finally have what I've always been aching for? Hum, let's see. Rocco can fuck me better than I ever dreamed of! Does he love me? I think we know that his heart will always truly belong to Angela. And Alex, the love of my life, is finally telling me that he wants to be with me. Does he love me? I think we know that he's an overachiever who hates to feel like he lost at anything. He's too ambitious for his own good. So although I do have two gorgeous men who claim to want me, I'm certainly not that girl on the cover of any romance novel. I was brought up believing that we should never judge a book by its cover. *So, so true.*

"I'm with Rocco now."

Alex reached over and took my hands in his. "You came into my life when you were having a very difficult time. I was too self-absorbed to understand that you were offering your love to me as a gift. I blew it then, and I blew it now. I know that Rocco is a good man. He knew how to give you what I couldn't. Briana, I'm ready now. I want you, and although I know that Rocco is a good man, well, he's just not the man for you. I am. I am the man for you, and you are the woman for me."

"Please don't say these things to me, not now. Alex, I've always loved you. I always will." Alex smiled, and he came in closer, about to kiss me.

"No. I will not do this. It's true that I love you. I feel so connected to you. You are in my heart, forever. Alex, if I had to create the perfect man, well, you'd be it! I think that I loved you even before I met you. I will always love you, and I don't think that I can change that. It's the most natural thing in the world for me to love you."

"OK, so what's wrong, then?"

"I also love Rocco, and I need him. He is a good man; you're right. He too came into my life when it was so difficult for me. I needed so much help. I felt so hopeless. And Rocco helped me, willingly and generously."

"I was stupid, but you can't be with a man because you're grateful to him."

"Grateful? Yes, I am grateful to him because he saved me from a sad, desperate, lonely place. But I also fell in love with him."

I really didn't want to hurt Alex, although he did deserve a little pain for all the tears that I'd cried for him. Being bitter is not a pretty look for me, and vengeance isn't so sweet after all. Not in this case, at least.

"It was actually very easy to love Rocco. I fell for him for being so good to me, and for wanting me. He wanted ME! I have nothing but my love to offer him. And he still just wanted ME! Grateful? Yes, of course I'm grateful to him. But I also love him."

In that moment I felt so angry with Alex, and with Peter, with life, and with everything.

"Why weren't you there for me, Alex? You didn't wait for me! You married Claire. I married Peter and I had a terrible life with him. You are my soul mate, but you weren't there for me. *You didn't wait for me.*"

Alex had a pained look in his eyes. It almost looked like he truly understood what I was saying, which is a little strange because it all sounded so crazy.

"Please, Alex. Understand me. I believe that you are my soul mate. And I appreciate where you're coming from, and how hard it was for you to say this to me. It hurts me because I just love you so much. But we can't be together, not now. Not in this lifetime. It's just not meant to be for us, not here and not now."

I was so tempted to mention the psychic that I had been seeing. I wanted to know if he felt the same way as I did. Did he feel the deep connection? Is it truly possible that the concept of "soul mates" is a real thing, and that Alex is mine and I am his? I always hated it when people would go on about their supposed soul mates, and then shortly after they would somehow come across their next "real" soul mate. How ridiculous! And yet, with Alex, I buy it. But it sounds so farfetched and naïve. These are the rantings of a lovesick schoolgirl, not a grown, mature woman.

"Briana…"

"Alex, I don't know how I know this, but I really believe that we'll find our way to each other one day. I don't know how, or where, or when, but it will happen. So trust that if we are meant to be together, it will happen for us somehow."

"That's right, Briana. I'm glad you realize that we are meant to be together. I'm inside of you now, my darling. I'm in your system. I'm in your blood, and I will be there forever. "

"Kinda like a virus, Alex? Or maybe more like an incurable disease?"

I really did mean what I said to Alex. I truly believe that we are soul mates, and that we will one day find our way to each other, even if it may be in another lifetime. I just don't know how I know it, and it doesn't make the pain of losing Alex any less real.

Rocco wasn't too happy that I went ahead and met with Alex. I guess I can't blame Rocco for being a little jealous. He does, after all, know that I love Alex. But I think that Rocco feels better about it now that our relationship is out in the open. So if Rocco is a little jealous about my love for Alex, does that mean that he must love me, even just a little? I think he does, even if he hasn't said the words yet. Why else would he want to be with me, want to spend time with my kids and pay for my expenses to try and make my life a little easier and stress-free?

Rocco soon went beyond the kindness he had already showed me when he paid for my new driveway and luxury appliances. Rocco knew that I was struggling to pay my line of credit at the bank. I didn't volunteer this information to him—I didn't want him to know about it. He was at my house when I received a phone call from the bank telling me that I was behind on a few payments and that it would affect my credit if I didn't make a payment soon. Well, I was beyond embarrassed, although it's not like I used the money to pay for frivolous things. I paid for bills, groceries, the mortgage...exciting things like that. You know how expensive life gets, even without luxuries. Not a half hour later, Rocco was on the phone with his bank, and arranged to have my credit cards paid, as well as my line of credit. He also told me that he would take care of my mortgage. That's when I told him that I really would not allow such a thing. He simply hugged me and told me that I shouldn't let my pride get in the way of a good thing.

"Briana, I know what it's like to worry about

money. I've been there. It's not your fault, and everyone has been there at one point or another. Just consider yourself lucky that you have me in your life." He said this with a huge grin on his face. "I've got the money, honey. I'm rich, you know! So let me do this because I can, and because it makes me happy."

I guess I should've resisted, but maybe I just didn't really want to that much. I really hate owing so much money. And honestly, I'd be the same way if I had a lot of money. I would be very generous with my loved ones, with charities and friends. I get it. It does hurt my ego a little, I'll admit, to be on the receiving end of all the help.

31

Green Is the Color of Hope

This was finally it. I was dying. I always thought that I would go in a more dignified way. But no, leave it to me to end my life in a humiliating way.

"Open your eyes, Briana! Don't miss this!"

"No! And I hate this! I hate you, Rocco!"

Rocco was laughing at me. He was on the zipline cable next to me, and we were flying over the city, side by side.

I can't believe that I let Rocco talk me into zip lining. We were in Montreal's Old Port, and although it is definitely a beautiful city, I don't need to see it from a bird's-eye view. But no, I had to listen to Rocco and go against every sane bone in my body that told me not to do it. So I was sliding down a cable, flying over the city of Montreal in a suspended harness. I'm afraid of heights.

"Open your eyes! Live, Briana! You're safe, so have some fun!"

I did open my eyes. Some people don't need to do extreme things to feel alive. I felt dead before I met Rocco. Feeling loved and wanted helped revive me. But now here I was, afraid of heights, and flying over my city with my legs dangling in the air. I opened my eyes, and then quickly closed them shut until it was over.

I felt a little angry with Rocco, although I understood that I shouldn't have been. In the few months that we were "an item," my life improved dramatically. Rocco brought love into my life as well as purpose and order.

What I should've been was afraid. The sick feeling in the pit of my stomach was familiar. I'd felt this ugly feeling before, when I first met Peter, as a young girl. I understood then, as I understand now, that something big was going to happen in my life. What I didn't understand back then was that the awful feeling in my stomach was really my instincts telling me that I was in for no good. I needed to run, and run like hell. But I was very young and naïve and I just brushed it off. This time around, I took my premonition very seriously and I felt a little anxious. However, I never in a million years could've imagined anything like this happening.

A couple of weeks later I was getting ready for a big gala event that Rocco and I were hosting for the Foundation. It was going to be the first big event that we would attend together, as a couple. Everyone was going to be there. Montreal's most affluent citizens were going to be in attendance, including our city's very own rock star surgeon.

As nervous as I was, I really went out of my way to make sure that I looked damn good! My evening gown was simple but chic, made of elegant chiffon that clung to my curves in just the right way. However, what made this gown so special was the color. It was a beautiful emerald green. For Italians, the color green represents hope, and many women choose to wear this color when they are celebrating a very special occasion, like when they get engaged to be married. I should mention that I didn't wear green at my engagement party. I wore a dark navy dress to celebrate the "joyous occasion."

Everyone looked so beautiful that night. Rocco looked so handsome in his elegant tux. Money really suits him! He wears it well.

Even Uncle Sal looked especially dapper this

evening, and it was obvious that he only had eyes for Zia Marina. The love that this elderly couple feels for each other is so clear to see, and it's so endearing.

Vincent and Maria seemed to be enjoying themselves. Their ballroom dance lessons were clearly paying off. Fred Astaire and Ginger Rogers would be jealous! OK, maybe not, but they just looked like they were having so much fun together.

Alex was there, of course. And, as usual, he looked great. He brought a date with him. She was tall, brunette, and beautiful. She looked a little like the Italian actress Monica Belucci. They made such a stunning couple; I couldn't help but admire that about them, although it also irritated me a little.

We had only been there a little over an hour. Not enough time when you're having fun. I could feel that it was a special night, so I really took it all in. The ballroom was so elegant, the food delicious, and the music intoxicating. I was in heaven, with my love. I felt so happy, so content. I remember it all, every detail, and nobody will ever take this away from me.

The shots could clearly be heard over the sound of the blazing music. I remember seeing Uncle Sal quickly make his way outside the ballroom doors. It was like he knew. Most were oblivious, but some had questioning looks on their faces. I didn't really think much of it, until I noticed that Rocco wasn't in the room. I stood there, frozen, while the dread slowly took over my body.

And then, somehow, I knew it too. It was Rocco. I don't know how I made it out of the ballroom. Rocco was lying on the floor. Uncle Sal was kissing Rocco's forehead. Some guy was on his cell, and told us that an ambulance was on its way.

I felt like I was in a dream. I was standing over Rocco's body. His beautiful face looked pale, but strangely peaceful. Maybe hearing Uncle Sal's anguished voice woke me from my trance. *"Figlio mio, figlio mio, figlio mio"* was what Uncle Sal repeatedly said. *Figlio mio*, my son.

"Rocco? Rocco?" I knelt down next to Rocco, on the floor, in a puddle of Rocco's blood. I reached for his hand and hugged it against my cheek. "Rocco, wake up, my love."

He just lay there. "Rocco! *Rocco! NO. Please, God, no."*

I was shaking my head, "No. No. No. Please, God? *Please."*

I kissed Rocco on the cheek. His face was so cold. His lips were colder. *But he's never cold.*

He wasn't waking up. I whispered in his ear, "Please wake up. I love you. I need you." I was quietly sobbing. I knew that he wasn't going to wake up.

The paramedics had arrived within minutes, but it was too late. Rocco was dead. His usually hot skin was as cold as ice. His lips had already lost their usual sensual curve, and they were hard. But he was still beautiful. He had a gunshot wound in his chest, and his tux was completely covered in blood. But he just looked like he was sleeping.

I stroked his hair and kept kissing him. His shirt was ruined. How stupid to think of such a thing. But Rocco really hated wearing anything that wasn't perfect. I remembered that time in his office when I dropped my Coke all over him and ruined his shirt. He immediately changed into a clean shirt. That was when we had our first kiss...

Rocco's upper body was cradled in my arms. He was my hero, my lover, my angel. But he had an angel of his own, and she obviously wanted him back with her.

Much later, after Rocco's body had already been brought to the morgue, I heard Maria try to comfort Uncle Sal and Zia Marina. She told them, "He's with Angela now." I don't think that she meant for me to hear it, because it was so painful to hear, so cruel and so true. Wasn't it enough that Angela already had his heart?

32

My Guardian Angel

I t's such a beautiful place. It's so peaceful here. There's always the sound of birds chirping in the background. Funny, up until now I really believed that there were birds in the mausoleum. I just realized that it must be a CD that they play because I also hear the sound of waves and, well, I'm not at the beach, am I?

Rocco was cremated, and I never saw him again after that day. I just refer to that day as "the day." It was supposed to be so special because it was our first official event as a real couple. I enjoy reliving most of the events of that day, but I do try not to obsess about what happened to Rocco— although I have to say that my dress of "hope" is still hanging on the closet door of my bedroom. It has Rocco's blood all over it. I can't get rid of it.

It has barely been a month since Rocco died. He was shot to death. The police apparently don't know who did it. But I know, and so does Uncle Sal. And we know why they did it. It was that god-forsaken book that Rocco wrote! Rocco got several warnings about not writing his tell-all book, but nobody could ever scare him off. He is, *was*, too strong and brave for that. Rocco's book will be published, and nobody could stop the truth from getting out. And I know that Rocco wouldn't have changed a single thing. Sadly, that book was also what initially brought Rocco into my life.

His ashes are in an urn, and they are kept in the family mausoleum at the cemetery up on the hill. It's such a beautiful place, and I try to visit several times a week. I know that my Rocco, "my rock," is not really here anymore, but somehow it helps me cope with his death when I visit his ashes.

I understand that life is truly about moments. If you're lucky and you've had many good moments, well then, good for you! Life can't be all good, and it can't be all bad. Although some people really do seem to be a little luckier than others. Obviously, if you're born in a safe, free, wealthy country during a good era, well, you're lucky and that's just that. What about those poor souls who have to endure life during times of war, or who are born in a developing country, or who face prejudice on a daily basis simply because of the color of their skin. I've been judged so many times because of where my parents emigrated from. But I still always felt very proud of my roots.

I guess I have to admit that I am one of the lucky ones in this life. I am lucky to have met Rocco and to have loved him, and be loved by him. Rocco and I have had many good moments together. My brief time with Rocco was filled with so many good times and they will always stand out for me in my life, and I will cherish them forever.

Sometimes I have images of Rocco and Angela together, hugging each other and laughing. They look so happy to me. I've really no doubt in my mind that Rocco is indeed in a better place now, with God, and with his true love. I do want him to be happy and in a good place, but I just miss him so much.

I do believe that I was *destined* to be born into life accidentally. I needed to be around to hold my mother's hand when she got cancer to tell her that she would be OK. Is it accidental that her illness is what inevitably led me into the arms of Alex, my soulmate? The planned births of Marco and Elisa depended on my accidental life, and the certain joy that their lives brought me made my existence worthwhile and essential. I would not have been blessed with the births of my children without having endured an unfavorable union with their father. Is it accidental that Peter is also responsible for the chance meeting with Rocco, who turned out to be a beautiful force in my life?

"I didn't mean to intrude. I'll come back another time if you like." It was Alex.

"No, don't go. You have as much a right to visit Rocco as I do. He was your friend."

"Yes, my friend. I just don't know how much of a good friend I was to him."

"Stop that, Alex. Rocco always thought of you as a good person, and he said as much, many times. Do you visit often?"

"No. I don't usually believe in this type of thing. I just really felt an overwhelming need to come here today."

"I find that I'm drawn here too. I know that he's not here, not really at least. But I like it here, you know?"

We stayed there together, with Rocco, for over an hour. It's funny, we didn't even talk much. It was getting late, and I needed to head back home.

"Briana, there's a great little Thai restaurant not too far from here. Let's grab some lunch."

Wasn't the Thai restaurant that Alex took me to on our first dinner date not too far from here?

"I don't think so, Alex."

"Oh, come on now." He looked at me, and I swear that I saw a sparkle in his eye. He grinned. "If not for me, then do it for the Foundation. I really need to discuss some matters with you that will benefit the Foundation."

He made me laugh. That was exactly how he got me to go out with him on that first date.

"OK, Alex. I guess I have to do what's best for the Foundation, right?"

I honestly don't think that Rocco would mind. He may even have somehow played a little role in this accidental meeting with Alex.

I turned one last time and looked at the shiny urn before leaving the mausoleum. I blew him a kiss. "Goodbye for now."

Alex took my hand and led me out, into the sunshine.

Made in the USA
Monee, IL
07 July 2026